M000306107

IT'S NOT ME, IT'S YOU

Young In Love Series

ELLE WRIGHT

Elle Wrights Books, LLC
Ypsilanti, Michigan
www.ElleWright.com

Editor:
Rhonda Merwarth
Rhonda Edits

Cover Design:
Sherelle Green

It's Not Me, It's You

I fake laugh every time I think about how ironic it is to be a commitment-phobe relationship therapist who is also the daughter of two world-renowned marriage and family counselors. Seriously, it's comical!

Want to know how I messed up my life? Getting arrested for stealing a priceless artifact for a tearful client.

Want to know what my biggest problem is? Spending my life teaching women how to break relationships when all I want to do is make a relationship—with him.

Want to know what that makes me? The Break-Up Expert who is questioning everything I thought I knew.

Dear Reader

Several years ago, one character changed everything for me. I didn't know much about her then. I only knew that she made a living helping people break up with their significant others. This character had a bunch of siblings, all named for soap opera characters. A world was formed, built around three close knit families—the Youngs, the Reids, and the Starks. A series was created, featuring eight very intelligent, very different siblings trying to find (or not) their one true love.

I'm super excited to finally be able to share this world and this family with you. Blake Young is something else! She's not that nice, but she's fiercely loyal. She's real, authentic. She's The Breakup Expert who's afraid of commitment.

I hope you enjoy her journey as much as I enjoyed writing it!

Love,
    Elle
    www.ellewright.com

Recommended Reading

MEET THE YOUNG FAMILY

It's Not Me, It's You is not the first book featuring a member of the Young Clan. If you'd like to get acquainted with this family before you read, I recommend starting with the following books:

First up, Paityn Young found everlasting love in my Park Manor novella, HER LITTLE SECRET. The twins, Blake and Bliss made their first appearance in her story.

Blake Young appeared again as Ryleigh's friend in my Once Upon a Baby novella, BEYOND EVER AFTER.

Duke Young burst onto the scene in my Pure Talent novels, THE WAY YOU TEMPT ME and THE WAY YOU HOLD ME. And he stole the show.

And, finally, Dallas Young made her presence known in my Once Upon a Funeral novella, FINDING COOPER.

www.ellewright.com

For my sisters, thank you for inspiring me to reach for the stars.

Trauma-Dicked

A BLAKE YOUNG ORIGINAL

Blake

June, Last Year

"**W**ell?" A soft smack to my ass followed the question, pulling me from a peaceful slumber.

I couldn't open my eyes, though. I couldn't even stretch like I normally did when I woke from a much-needed nap. If I did either or both of those things, I'd give myself away. Because there was a man behind me, a penis inside me. And I'd actually fallen asleep—during sex. *There's a first for everything*.

Things had seemed promising tonight. Tasty food, sensual music, stimulating conversation. Dr. Donell Pointer had hit all my superficial checkmarks for consent. *Looks*.

Sincere brown eyes, pretty white teeth, strong body. *Voice*. He sounded like hot sex on a smooth, dark chocolate stick. *Personality*. The good doctor had charisma. I'd laughed at his jokes and had even enjoyed a debate on why soulmates didn't exist. Of course, he'd landed on the they-do side of the fence, while I'd stayed firmly on the no-the-hell-they-don't side. I wasn't one of those women… I didn't believe in soulmates or that love-at-first-sight bullshit. The only way to fully love someone was if you *knew* them. Fight me. But even though he was a sappy son of a bitch, it was okay. Because he'd earned a check in my most important wet-panties category. *Smile*. Oh. My. God. That thing lit up the room. And the tiny creases around his full lips made my decision easy. Sex. All night, preferably. But at least two times.

Except, I couldn't get through *one* time without a smidge of drool on the pillow, and not because he'd knocked me out with his prowess. Dr. Donnell was defi-nitely fine as hell. Too bad he had no fuck game. No back-breaking. No tongue-talking. No toe-curling orgasm. If brown liquor was the devil, there had to be a worse name for bad, boring, small-ass dick. Hell? Disappointment? Underwhelming? No, tragic? Yep, that's it.

"Blake?" His low voice broke my reverie.

Sighing, I opened my eyes slowly. *Damn*. Such a shame to be so hot, yet so limp. A nod and a forced smile later, I rolled over on my back and tried not to look at his *little* problem. "Where is my…?" I spotted my dress on the floor near the door. Before I could slide off the bed and race toward the bathroom, his hand wrapped around my wrist.

"Baby, where do you think you're going? I'm not done with you."

Oh, boy. I couldn't help the hard roll of my eyes. *Lord, I promise to do better and not be a hoe if you'll just get me out of here without me having to hurt this man's feelings.* He was a friend of a friend of an associate. The last thing I needed was friend-group gossip. "I have to leave. Early meeting." I offered him another smile and a light caress on his cheek.

He pulled me closer and nuzzled his nose against my neck. "How about you stay? We can have breakfast in the morning. Together."

Shit. He just said the magic, dirty word. *Together* was not what's up. "No need. I really have to go." I slipped out of his arms. But that hand of his remained on my wrist.

"I want to see you again. Maybe you'll give me a chance to change your mind about soulmates."

Like hell. "Not likely," I grumbled. "So, about that." I scratched my head, scrambled to find the right words. Somehow, "fuck off" seemed too harsh. "We don't have to do this. If you haven't realized yet, I'm not one of those women who needs the obligatory 'let's get together soon' speech." Shrugging, I continued, "It's probably best if we just not even try."

"Blake, you're a beautiful woman."

Can he just shut the hell up?

"I had a good time with you tonight." He brushed his thumb over my nipple.

I really have to find my panties.

Donnell rubbed his nose over my cheek and placed a chaste kiss there. "I don't want this to end."

Okay, I can live without my panties.

A mix between a groan and a whimper escaped his lips as he cupped my pussy in his palm—his *small* palm.

How the hell didn't I notice this?

"You're so beautiful," he whispered against my ear. "I want you."

Fuck the panties and the bra. I gripped his hand before his

3

finger made contact with my clit. "Okay, stop. I'm done here." I pushed him away, stood, and picked up my dress.

"Blake?"

I rolled my eyes, slipping my dress on quickly. Luckily I'd chosen the comfortable, flowy maxi dress over the sexy, short black dress I'd considered wearing. Turning to him, I met his waiting, pitiful gaze. "Dr. Pointer, thanks for tonight. But I'm not interested in more of this." I motioned toward the bed. "It was…" I stopped short of saying it was nice, because I made it a habit not to lie. "Thanks for dinner and the…conversation."

Bolting from the room, I slammed the door shut and leaned against it to catch my breath. I ran my fingers through my probably fucked-up hair and hurried out of the hotel.

THE NEXT MORNING, I snuck into my office, hoping to avoid—

"Blake!"

Shit.

My sister, Dallas, barged into my office and took a seat while I pretended to work. "Girl, stop. You're not working. I saw your ass sneaking in here like a thief in *my* five-inch stilettos and *my* pencil skirt. Which I want back as soon as you take that shit to the cleaners."

I shrugged. "Well, it's been a few months. I figured you didn't want them anymore."

"Don't play me." She crossed her legs and assessed me.

I ducked my head. "Stop looking at me like that."

Frowning, Dallas said, "I don't know why you look different today." She tapped her chin. "Your makeup is on point, hair combed… You're fly in my clothes. But your

4

eyes are giving me a strong you-fucked-up vibe. What the hell is wrong with you?"

That was the million-dollar question. After I'd left the doctor last night, I'd spent an exhausting amount of time questioning myself, my actions, my judgment. Which was new. Dick was a dime a dozen, and I'd perfected the art of getting mine while remaining a lady. But lately…something felt off.

Maybe it was my job? No, I loved what I did. I helped women take control of their lives. And I did that by encouraging them to lose the dead weight—that man who asked to borrow money every week because he gambled his entire paycheck, the cheater who blamed it on his pain, the jerk who thought he was entitled to beat his wife or girl-friend into submission. I assisted with the breakup, whether it was a smothering idiot, an annoying mama's boy, a scrub boyfriend, or even a friend-with-benefits who wouldn't accept that the enrollment period was over. I'd seen it all.

I couldn't help but wonder, though, if my experience had fucked me up in the head or something. How else could I explain my recent track record with men?

"Before you answer that…where the hell were you last night?" Dallas asked, pulling me from my thoughts. "And why was I the only one helping Mom cook for Asa's gradu-ation party? I called you three times. I thought we talked about this—answer my damn calls. I don't care if your ass is getting dicked down by Idris Elba. If I call you, pick up the phone."

Groaning, I leaned back in my seat and stared at the ceiling. "Dallas, stop. If you'd just shut up and let me get a word in, I'll tell you where I was."

Although Dallas wasn't the oldest of my siblings, she certainly held the bossy title. My sissy was an attorney, specializing in the business of marriage. Her billable hours were spent negotiating prenuptial agreements and brokering mergers between people willing to walk down the aisle and promise to love, honor, and obey in order to enhance their bottom lines. We worked together, sharing office space in Ann Arbor with my twin, Bliss, and our brother, Dexter. While our careers were different, our businesses complemented each other perfectly. It made sense to purchase the building together. Plus, I enjoyed being close to my family.

Dallas folded her arms over her chest, arching a brow. "Okay. Talk."

"It was the doctor," I confessed.

"Huh? What doctor?"

I met her gaze. "Dr. Pointer? My date last night."

"Oh, you mean the date you'd promised to ditch so we could peel potatoes with Mom?"

"Dallas!" I shouted. "I'm sorry about the damn potatoes, shit." Sighing, I stood and paced the room. "I'm rethinking a lot of things."

"Really? So you like this doctor?"

Pausing, I whirled around. "Hell. No." I rolled my eyes. "If lying on your dick was a person…"

Her mouth fell open. "Get out. The D was trash?"

"Girl…I can't even describe how bad it was." I cringed, thinking about the experience. "I just know I don't want the doctor to see me now—or ever again."

"Damn." She shook her head. "He's so fine. That's tragic."

"I fell asleep."

Dallas blinked. "Da fuq? While he was doing it to you?"

"Yes. Drooling and everything."

My sister barked out a laugh so loud, she nearly toppled on the floor. Then, I started laughing too. Which was exactly what I needed in that moment. I sat down on the love seat near the window. Dallas patted her chest. "I can't…" She cleared her throat. "I have to get it together." She snorted, then smacked a hand over her mouth. "I have to tell Paityn and Bliss."

The sex therapist and the matchmaker. Hm. Yeah, no. "If you call anyone, I'll burn this skirt and toss these shoes into the Detroit River."

Waving a dismissive hand, Dallas pulled out her phone. Seconds later, a text popped up in our Sissy Group. Before I could stand up and choke Dallas, messages started coming through in rapid succession. All of them full of laughing and facepalm emojis.

I turned my phone over. "I hate you," I announced.

Dallas winked. "You love me."

I threw a pillow at her. "You get on my nerves."

"This is what sisters are for." She shrugged. "If we can't laugh at you, who can?"

Giggling, I sighed. "Seriously, Dallas. I feel a little unsettled right now."

My sister stopped typing on her phone and glanced over at me. Tilting her head, she walked to the love seat and sat down next to me. "I hope you know this skirt is tight as hell and I probably won't be able to get back up without assistance."

Laying my head on her shoulder, I said, "What if I'm broken?"

"Because of some bad dick?"

"No, fool." I shoved her lightly, then dropped my head back on her shoulder. "Things have been weird for me since I broke up with Corny Colton."

Boyfriends weren't my thing. But I'd gone against all of my instincts and let Colton Drake call me his girl. Somehow, that one little concession on my part had morphed

7

into meeting the family, going on trips, and calling each other multiple times a day.

Dallas grinned. "I loved Colton."

It wasn't just Dallas. All *seven* of my siblings liked Colton. Even Tristan. And my oldest brother didn't like anyone. My parents loved him too. My father respected him, and my mother had already picked out our china pattern.

Rolling my eyes, I muttered, "I know."

The problem was *I* didn't like him that much. Yes, I loved having sex with him. He was good-looking, intelligent, successful. But that was about it. He didn't make me laugh; he didn't challenge me. I couldn't imagine spending another minute with him, let alone a lifetime. Not that I was looking for a soulmate. I wasn't. *And I'm not.*

"There was no substance. No…" I struggled to find the right word. "I don't know. Honestly, I think it was his dick."

Dallas chuckled. "Blake!"

"I'm so serious," I said. "It was the bomb. I couldn't stop wanting it."

"Well—" she sighed, "—I know the feeling."

I glanced up at her. "Really? Is there something you want to tell me?"

"Nope," she chirped. "We're talking about you."

"I think I've made a decision. I'm putting myself on punishment."

"From what?"

"Yak and dick."

Dallas scooted away and pinned me with a gaze. Raising a skeptical brow, she asked, "What?"

"Dark liquor is of the devil."

"Bullshit. Cognac is a gift to be freely enjoyed. Responsibly."

Giggling, I said, "You're a nut. Anyway, I can do this. No more Colton and his magic dick, or the doctor and his tragic dick. And no more Hennessy. I need to get my life together."

"I don't believe it. There is no way... You can't *not* have sex."

"I'm not really a hoe, Sissy," I crowed.

She smiled. "I never said you were. But you've always enjoyed sex—without the relationship. And there's nothing wrong with that as long as you're safe. Men do that shit all the time."

"Still, I feel like I need an intervention and an intermission."

"So, what is this?" she asked. "Are you feeling like you want to settle down? Maybe have a boyfriend?"

I glared at her. "Hell no. I don't need those types of problems."

"Okay. I don't understand, but you do you." Dallas struggled to get up. Grinning, I stood and pulled her to her feet. "Who knows? Maybe this will be good for you."

"I agree."

The door flew open and my twin, Bliss, stormed in. Without a word, she plopped down on the same love seat. Dallas and I exchanged glances. Tears filled Bliss' eyes, and I rushed over to her, while Dallas grabbed the box of Kleenex off my desk.

"Weren't you just laughing at my expense in our text group? What's wrong?" I asked.

Bliss sniffled. "Everything. But you're still crazy as hell for falling asleep during sex. I needed that laugh."

I brushed a strand of hair from her forehead. "What's going on? I can't help if I don't know."

"*We* can't help if *we* don't know?" Dallas joined us on

the love seat and handed her the tissue. "Besides, we don't cry in the office, boo. You know that."

"Is it Tyler?" I asked. "Because if I have to beat his ass, I will. I've been waiting for the chance." Bliss had been with Tyler for years. I'd tried everything to get her to wake up and see he wasn't shit. Unlike Colton, no one liked that asshole. Yet, Bliss had stayed with him.

Wiping her nose, Bliss gave me a sidelong glance. "We got into a fight."

I tensed. Closing my eyes, I whispered, "Please tell me he didn't hit you."

She averted her gaze and shook her head.

"Why am I not convinced?" I asked.

While I'd never known Tyler to use physical violence, I'd noticed the way he'd spoken to my sister over the years, the subtle jabs about her appearance, his criticism of everything Bliss had done for herself. My sister was a bad-ass boss, a multi-millionaire in the making, the owner of a specialized matchmaking business with a slew of happily married clients. It was high time for her to leave her dud behind.

"He didn't hit me," Bliss assured.

Dallas rubbed Bliss' back. "What is it, then?"

"We broke up," she cried. "This time for good."

I locked eyes with Dallas, nodding at the mental high five she'd just given me. "Aw," I said, mentally slapping myself for not even bothering to sound sincere. "Well, Bliss, maybe it's time to move on."

"He cheated on me!" she groaned between sobs. "For three years."

"What?" Dallas and I shouted at the same time.

"Three years?" I asked. Tyler was an asshole, but... damn. "How did you find out?"

"Did he tell you?" Dallas asked.

Bliss plopped her head on Dallas' shoulder. "I saw him with her—and their two kids."

"Two kids?" Dallas leaned back.

I stood up. "What the hell? You know what? I'm kicking his black ass. All up and down the street. I might even stab his trifling behind with the heel of Dallas' shoe," I muttered.

Bliss' hand on my wrist stopped me from grabbing my purse and hightailing it over to their house. "Blake, don't."

I counted to ten before looking at her. "What? If you're about to make an excuse for his sorry ass—"

"Blake," Dallas warned, shaking her head. "As much as I want to grab my sword and join you at the house, she doesn't need this right now."

Taking in a deep breath, I turned to her. "Fine. What else aren't you telling us?"

"I'm pregnant."

Chapter 1

SHIT DAMN MOTHER FUCKER

Blake

January, This Year

*a*t fifteen, I'd started sipping on my father's cognac while they were out of town. I blamed that shit on my older brother, Duke. He'd always been a bad influence on me. That same year, I'd lost my virginity to an older boy, Keon Pollard. I blamed that shit on myself, because... well, I just liked it.

Basically, I've been fucking and drinking over half of my life. Now, at thirty-one, I was dry—literally and figuratively. Granted, it was my own decision to stop having sex and drinking that good brown liquor, but it'd been over six freakin' months. "Horny and thirsty" only scratched the surface of my emotional bandwidth. Add grumpy, frustrated, angry, snippy, sad, melancholy, concerned, exhausted, and we might be getting somewhere. On most days, I could handle myself and everyone around me. But today?

"Duke! You drank all my Berry Punch!" I slammed the refrigerator door. To my right, ready to go out in the recycle bin was my once-full carton.

The only thing I needed every morning was a small glass of Berry Punch. It was my morning routine, something I looked forward to since I didn't drink soft drinks or Kool-Aid or anything other than water, the occasional cup of coffee, and booze. And, *dammit*, I wanted my juice!

I grabbed the empty carton from the counter, stalked to the second guest bedroom, and barged in. An unfamiliar yelp caught me off guard, and I flicked the light on. In the bed, Duke and some woman were wrapped around each other.

"Ugh! Get out of my house!" I pitched the carton and lopped Duke on the forehead.

"Ouch," he grumbled, rubbing his temple. "Shit."

Scooping up a mound of clothes off the floor, I tossed it on the stranger's head. "Now." The woman scrambled to gather her things and hightailed it out of the room. I turned my ire on my brother.

Unbothered, he burrowed into a pillow. "Thanks for the save, B. I needed a way out of that."

It wasn't uncommon for any of us to serve as an excuse for my playboy brother to ditch a date. But this wasn't one of those times. "You too, punk. It's time for you to go." Turning on my heels, I stomped out of the room, nearly bumping into my very pregnant twin. "Shit," I hissed. "I need to get out of here."

Bliss winced, rubbing her belly. "I think I might be in

labor," she groaned. "I've been feeling contractions for the last hour."

I rolled my eyes and let out a heavy sigh. "You're not in labor, Sissy. The doctor told you last night it was Braxton-Hicks." *And the night before that, and the week before that.* We'd been to the hospital at least four times over the past ten days, and the five hours we'd spent there yesterday had worn me out. "Did you do what Dr. Love suggested? Drink water? Go for a walk? Maybe you should come to the office today. It might help to keep your mind off everything."

Bliss pouted. "It hurts, though. Can you take me to the hospital again?"

"No." Brushing past her, I headed toward the kitchen. I loved my sister. Really. But going to the hospital wasn't an option. I had shit to do. Like be by myself. My house had been invaded by siblings. Bliss had moved in after breaking up with Tyler. Duke had been in town since New Year's Day. And while I enjoyed my brother's company most times, I was sick and tired of him eating my damn food and drinking all of my freakin' juice. *Ugh.*

Bliss joined me in the kitchen a few seconds later. "Are you mad at me?"

I counted to ten. Then, counted to ten again. "No, boo." I gave her my best almost-smile. "I'm just tired. Can you tell Duke to get out when he wakes up?" Opening the refrigerator, I searched for something to eat on the way to work. Unfortunately, the only thing appetizing was an apple. Muttering a curse, I grabbed it and tossed it into my bag. Luckily, Dexter was in charge of food this week at the office, which meant we'd get good, hot food instead of the bland, healthy food Dallas always brought. "I'm running late."

As I moved through the house, I managed to avoid eye

contact with Bliss. She was my kryptonite. Perhaps it was the twin thing, but she was the *only* one of my siblings who had the power to make me change my entire day around to help her. The last several months with her were all the proof anyone needed. I'd gone to doctor appointments, shopped for baby shit, held her hand during ultrasounds, lotioned her feet when she couldn't reach them, and planned a damn gender reveal party.

"Blake?" Bliss called.

"Damn, B, you need to stop acting like a virgin and get some," Duke grumbled as he entered the living room. Picking up a pillow, he grinned at me. "Punch this. It might help with that tension in your shoulders."

Glaring at my brother, I punched *him* instead—in the gut. I smirked when he doubled over and fell back on the couch. "Ooh, that felt good."

"You sneaked me." He blew out a harsh breath. "I taught you better than that."

"You also taught me not to take shit from anyone. That includes you, asshole." I put on my coat. "You know, I like living alone. But every night this week, I've had company. I'm putting my foot down. I need my space back." Bliss opened her mouth to speak, but I rushed on, "Not you, Sissy." Addressing Duke again, I added, "Aside from Bliss, no one is allowed over for the next two weeks."

"You're kicking me out?" Duke stood, a frown on his face. "Seriously?"

"Yes. You had sex in my house!" I smacked him on his shoulder. "In. My. House." I shoved him back down on the couch. "No one has sex in this house but me! Get out. Go to Dex's house. Or Dallas'." The triplets were close, but Duke always insisted on staying with me when he was in town. "I don't care where you go. Hell, there are six other houses you can go to."

Duke exchanged a worried glance with Bliss. Lifting his hands up, he said, "Fine. But I'm concerned about you. Maybe you need to go to the dojo and hit something harder."

"He's right, Sissy," Bliss said. "You've been on a terror the last few days."

I took a deep breath and let it out slowly. "I'm fine. Go for a walk around the block with Duke, then take a warm bath. If it doesn't ease your contractions, call me."

"I'll cook dinner tonight," Duke offered. My brother's reputation as a talented chef had been earned. He could throw down in the kitchen, but I didn't want anything from him in that moment. "And I'll buy you three cartons of Berry Punch."

I snatched my purse and bag off the table. "And eggs, bottled water, chicken, salmon, cereal, and cheese! Eating all my shit." I smacked him one more time for good measure. "You're still leaving today." Without another word, I walked out.

The twenty-minute drive to work consisted of me trying to find my peace and my peace flying out the window every time my mother called to tell me something about the baby shower.

"Mom, I'm at the office. I'll call you later," I said. "Promise. Love you."

I dropped my phone in my purse and rushed into the building. *Hopefully, the rest of my day is uneventful.*

Unfortunately, I wasn't that lucky, because this fool... "Get your punk ass out of here!" I growled.

Tyler stood, blocking the entrance to our suite of offices. "Where's Bliss? She's usually the first one in the office."

"I don't believe I stuttered." I shoved him aside, pulled out my key, and unlocked the door.

"Blake, come on. I need to talk to her."

When he started to follow me inside, I stopped and turned to him. Raising a challenging brow, I said, "Give me a reason." I dropped my bag on a chair near the door. "I promised my sister I wouldn't do anything rash or violent to you, but cross this threshold. *Please*."

I'd always been a fighter. As kids, I fought all of Bliss' battles with whatever I could find, but most often with my feet or fists. Which was why my parents enrolled me in karate at a young age—to teach me discipline. The moment I learned my first stance was the moment that had changed everything. I'd spent years training with my award-winning sensei, earning my black belt at sixteen and competing in tournaments around the world. Lately, the demands of my business had kept me away from the dojo, but unfortunately for Tyler, I was ready to take out my frustrations on him. Seven months of pent-up frustration, with no head to crack or dick to ride… I needed an outlet.

"She's having my baby," Tyler sneered. "I'll take her to court to get what's mine."

"Is that a threat?" Cracking my knuckles, I pinned him with a glare. "And what exactly is *yours*? I'm curious. Which girlfriend and kid are you claiming today?"

"Your family can't keep me away from my baby."

Technically, it wasn't my *family* who kept him from Bliss. It was the threat of feeling one of my brother's fists against his jaw. I let out a slow breath. This day could go to hell. "Do you really want to do this, Tyler? Because I got time today."

He backed away, hands up. *The lil' punk.* "I'm just sayin'. She can't do this to me."

"Obviously, you didn't think about that before you went off and had a whole 'nother family while my sister was supporting your broke ass."

"If she would've let me explain, then I—"

I laughed. "Explain? You tried it, muthafucka. Wrong sister. You already know I'm not about that bullshit, so you should've left when you realized Bliss wasn't here."

Despite an overwhelming amount of evidence, including paternity tests and screenshots sent courtesy of his *other* girlfriend, Tyler had acted like he hadn't done anything wrong. He'd maintained that he was the victim of Bliss and her need to get married when he hadn't been ready. He'd blamed my sister for making him cheat on her. At this point, the baby was an afterthought. He hadn't attended a single pre-natal appointment, no Lamaze class, and hadn't even shown up for the gender reveal. He just wanted Bliss back under his thumb. He wanted *her* beautiful self on his arm, *her* talent, *her* connections, *her* business, and *her* money.

"Listen, Blake, I—"

I pointed at him. "No, you listen. The—"

"Auntie, B!"

I glanced toward the elevators. My niece, Raven, waved as her eyes darted back and forth between me and Tyler. Normally, the presence of my niece wouldn't have deterred me from cussing Tyler out, but she wasn't alone. One of her friends stood behind her.

Smiling at her, I said, "Hey, baby girl. Give me a second." When she nodded, I turned my attention back to Tyler. "The next time you decide to come to *my* office, think twice. Stay away from me. Stay away from my sister. Get out."

"Everything okay, Auntie?" Raven approached us timidly. "Is Aunt Bliss okay?"

I wrapped my arms around her. "I'm fine. So is Bliss. He's leaving." Shooting Tyler one last glare, I ushered both girls inside the suite and slammed the door in his face. "What brings you my way?" I asked, picking up my things.

"You look tense," Raven said. "Like you wanted to smack him."

"That's an understatement," I muttered.

"Give me a sec," she told her friend. "I want to talk to my aunt alone first."

As I headed to my office, I flicked on lights, opened blinds, and straightened the pillows on the sofas. It was very rare that I arrived to the office first. Bliss was the early bird of my big clan, while I typically ran ten to fifteen minutes late to everything—by design. Because I'd learned early on that the first one there or up always had to cut the vegetables or peel the potatoes for my mother. And I hated that shit.

Raven plopped down on one of my chairs. "I need some advice, Auntie."

Eyeing her, I asked, "Are you good? Haven't seen you in a while."

Nodding, Raven said, "I'm fine. Been working a lot."

"Good. And dorm life?"

She grinned. "I love living on campus."

"I'd love living in the dorm too, if your daddy was my daddy."

"Auntie!" She laughed, setting her phone on the desk. "I love my dad."

"I love him too," I told her. "But we don't call him a fun-killer for nothing."

And my oldest brother had always been that way. When we were kids, Tristan had made my home life hell. Seriously. Like, pure torture. His overprotective, overbearing, overreacting ass stayed making me miserable. For years, I couldn't buy a date, because he'd threatened everyone who'd dared to call the house for me. It had almost felt like he had a personal vendetta against me. Until I'd discovered he'd done the same thing to all of us girls. Of course, I loved him. But I'd be lying if I said I hadn't done a little cheer when he'd enlisted and shipped out. Although I'd hated the thought of him fighting overseas, I enjoyed the freedom.

"Anyway, what's up?" I took my seat and powered up my laptop. "Is it guy advice?"

"Sort of," she admitted with a shrug.

I took in her features, catalogued her body language—the way she nibbled on her bottom lip, the slight tremble in her hands. "Raven? Do I have to beat someone's ass? I been ready."

Twenty years ago, we were all surprised when Tristan had announced he was going to be a father. Especially since he was so young and he'd always been the one to say he'd never wanted to have a kid of his own.

Yet, when Raven had entered our lives, with her dark curls and puffy cheeks, I'd been immediately smitten. Since then, I'd made it a point to be a part of her life, even though she'd mostly lived in Virginia with her mother. Every summer, every spring break, and every other Christmas, she'd spent with us. And when she'd graduated from high school, she'd made the decision to attend my alma mater, University of Michigan in Ann Arbor, so she could be near us.

"Auntie?"

Raven's voice pulled me back to the moment. "Yes?"

"You remember my friend Dory, don't you?"

I smirked. "Nemo's bestie?"

Giggling, she shook her head. "You're hilarious. But no."

"I'm just playin'. That's her out in the lobby, right?"

"Yes." Raven smiled. "She's been such a good to friend to me, and I wanted to return the favor."

Raven was in her second year at the university, and I'd met at least twenty of her friends. Dory was the dud of the group, the quiet, sneaky type I usually didn't like. "So this advice is for Dory?" I asked. "Not you?"

"She's in a bad situation," Raven explained. "I told her I'd ask you to help her."

I frowned. "Are you sure you have the right Aunt? You know I'm not that nice."

"I know who I'm talking to, Auntie."

I sighed. "Fine. Help her how?"

Raven sucked in a deep breath. "There's this professor…" She folded her arms across her chest. "Professor Cole. African-American Studies."

"Okay?" It wasn't like Raven to beat around the bush. She got that from our side of the family. The fact that she seemed hesitant set off alarms. "Is she flunking?"

Shaking her head, Raven said, "She's definitely not passing the class."

I shrugged. "Not sure what I can do about that. Maybe Dallas can help negotiate some makeup work or something."

"They're sleeping together," Raven blurted out.

Oh, boy.

"He's taking advantage of her," she continued. "He kicked her out of the class in front of everyone. That's how we all found out. She confessed everything and showed us the text messages." Raven leaned forward, whispering, "She even had a dick pic."

I wasn't sure what I'd expected, but this was definitely not it. The last thing I wanted to do was step into a profes-

sor-student situation. *Been there, done that.* "I still don't understand why you need me," I told her. "If anything, this feels
like a legal issue."

"We discussed your article during one of our women's
empowerment meetings."

The last year had been a whirlwind for me. I'd penned
an article entitled, "It's Not Me, It's You." It had gone
viral, earning me a ton of new fans and my fair share of
enemies. Mostly bitter men. What had started as a simple
letter to women who blamed themselves for the deterioration of their relationships had ended with talk show
appearances, speaking engagements, book deals, and a
slew of job offers.

"She knows you're The Breakup Expert," Raven
added.

That nickname had followed me from elementary
school—when I'd done Janet King a favor by dumping
stinky Hugh Frank during morning recess—to now. And
I'd used that name and skillset to build my brand.

I smirked. "Does she know I'm not that nice? If she's
looking for someone to hold her hand while she cries, I'm
not the one."

Raven sighed heavily. "I just want her to be okay. She's
not herself."

I met my niece's concerned gaze. Standing, I walked
around my desk and stopped in front of her. "Baby girl, I
know you're worried about your friend. But, if I'm being
honest, this sounds a little farfetched."

"Why do you say that?"

Hunching a shoulder, I explained, "Because sometimes
young, impressionable women make up things in their
head. Especially if a professor is handsome or serves as a
father surrogate or reminds them of someone back home."

"He's hot, though. A lot of us—" Raven cleared her throat. "I mean, them…" She scratched the back of her neck. "Trust me, a lot of the women at my school wouldn't mind doing him."

I arched a questioning brow. "Really? Is he a teaching assistant?"

"No."

"Fine professor" felt like an oxymoron. I'd only known *one* in my lifetime. "How old is he?"

"He's your age." She picked up her phone and typed something. A few seconds later, she held it up so I could see his picture. "It's not a good pic. He looks way better in person. Disarming."

Taking the phone from her, I studied the man. Brown skin, light brown eyes, chiseled face, serious expression, stuffy suit. He wasn't bad on the eyes, but he wasn't blow-your-mind fine, either. "I don't get it. He's bland to me. Definitely not someone I'd risk my collegiate career on."

Raven took her phone away from me. "You don't understand. This pic does him no justice."

"Whatever you say," I said.

"He's so knowledgeable."

"Well, he *is* a professor," I retorted. "I'd expect him to be intelligent."

"And he challenges us to do more for our communities, to learn more about our history. His Hip Hop and Sociology class is the best class I've taken! Other universities are trying to woo him away, but he won't leave, because his family is here."

I frowned. "Are you sure your *friend* is the one who has the crush on him?"

"I'm sure, Auntie." Raven flashed sad eyes at me. "Please? Can you at least talk to her?"

Sighing, I told her to go get Dory. A few minutes later, both of them stepped into my office. "Hi, Dory." I motioned for her to take a seat. "What can I do for you?"

"I'm in love with my professor."

That one statement let me know Dory wasn't here to end her relationship. "Does your professor love *you?*" I asked.

Dory glanced at Raven, who gestured for her to continue. "He told me he did."

I assessed Dory. The young lady was kind of attractive in a sweet sort of way. Beautiful skin, hair, and nails. She wore mom jeans, an oversized sweatshirt, and sneakers. Yet, nothing about her screamed *have-a-torrid-affair-with-a-professor* type. Now, if we'd been talking about having an affair with a life-sized mannequin…

"Ms. Young, I know this may seem weird. But I'm shy. Professor spoke to the quiet part of me. One night after class, we went for coffee. Then, he took me to his place."

The story was familiar, but still… "What are you looking to do here, sweetheart? I'm not opposed to listening and helping you walk away from a harmful situation, but you have to be ready. There's so much wrong with this picture. Starting with the fact that he's your professor."

"He kicked me out of his class," she said.

Folding my arms over my chest, I pinned her with a stern glare. "Raven told me. But what do *you* want to do?"

Silence.

"Dory, tell her what you told me," Raven prodded. "She needs to know."

When she didn't say anything for a minute, I stood. "How about you come back when you actually want to talk? I have a pretty busy day."

"What would you do if someone older and handsome

and charismatic paid you attention that you'd never had before?" Dory asked.

I swallowed as uncomfortable memories flashed through my mind. "Listen, we've all been there." It was my patented line. I usually led with it when I met new clients. This time, though, I wanted to throw up. "But this is not an average situation. Your accusations are huge, not just for his career but for yours. You have to decide what *you* want to do and how far *you* want to take this."

"I know we'll probably never be together. I just want to graduate on time," Dory said, a tear falling from her eyes. "I received a letter from the Dean. He's ruining my name. They want to kick me out of the school."

Heat flushed through my body as anger, hot and dark, welled up inside. Dory didn't need to say anything else. As far as I was concerned, Professor Cole was already guilty. I'd been on the receiving end of an attempt to ruin my reputation and I wouldn't wish that on anyone.

"He won't even let me walk away from him with my dignity," she continued. "And he's keeping all my stuff at his place."

With narrowed eyes, I asked, "How much time did you spend at his house?"

Dory shrugged. "I don't know. Months."

"Are we talking clothes, electronics…?"

"Both. I left my grandmother's vase and a painting there. They're both priceless, worth thousands of dollars."

Logically, I knew sometimes it was best to leave everything behind to get away from a harmful boyfriend. But I wanted her to get her belongings back. It was the principle. Yes, she was a consenting adult, but that damn professor knew better. He'd used his position to entrap her in a one-sided relationship. He deserved a foot up his ass. *Disgusting piece of shit.*

"Please, help me," she pleaded.

AN HOUR LATER, Dory had run off, leaving me literally clutching a vase as a police cruiser zoomed into the driveway of Professor Cole's home. "Deep shit" was an understatement. My black ass was going to jail. *Fuck.*

Chapter 2

911

Lennox

One Hour Ago

"*M*arry me?"

Something was very wrong here. I glanced around at the building crowd in the restaurant. All attention was on me—the amused stares from the group of brothas picking up their carry-out near the cash register, the wide eyes of the older women in the corner booth across from us, the open mouths of the waitresses, the raised brow of my best friend, the furious glares from my sisters, and the hostess sneaking a glance when she should've been working. Then, there was the woman, kneeling down in front of me, holding up a diamond band.

The tentative smile on Ayana's lips, her quivering chin, let me know she was nervous. She should've been.

I considered myself a progressive person. Really. Whenever the topic of women popping the question came up in discussion, I'd often shrugged it off and gave a gracious response about women making boss moves—or some shit like that. But I never assumed I'd be in this position myself, being proposed to in the middle of my favorite breakfast spot.

"Annoyed" was an understatement. Because not only would I have to embarrass Ayana in front of all these people, I wasn't sure I'd be able to come back here without being labeled *that* guy, the asshole who'd broken an innocent woman's heart in public. No one in the establishment knew she *wasn't* innocent. They didn't know the hell she'd put me through while we'd been together and after we'd broken up— a year ago. They wouldn't understand the toll that relationship had had on my credit after she'd taken out credit cards in my name to fund her gambling habit. They couldn't fathom the emotional havoc she'd wreaked in my life; the tears I'd had to watch my mother shed when Ayana had pawned my grandmother's ring. No, they didn't get it, but I didn't care.

Vaughn cleared his throat, drawing my attention from Ayana. He gripped my younger sister, Emerie's, hand. "Bruh? I don't want my baby to go to jail today."

Last year, Emerie had surprised us all when she'd announced she was moving to Los Angeles to be with Vaughn. While I would never have picked my best friend for my little sister, they were good for each other. They'd both been through a lot, and I was glad they were happy. The day had started out good enough with their arrival in town for a wedding. With my luck lately, I should've known it wouldn't last.

I glanced at Emerie, then at my older sister, Dana. The murderous look in their eyes told me I needed to handle my business before one or both of them pulled their earrings off and took care of it for me.

Letting out a heavy sigh, I grumbled. "Get up, Ayana."

"Len?" The smile on her face fell as she stood. She set the ring on the table. "Please."

"What the hell are you doing?" I said, keeping my voice low.

"Baby?" Ayana grabbed my hand. "I want to take our relationship to the next level. We talked about marriage. Let's do it."

Marrying her would've been the mistake of a lifetime. Instinctively I'd known that for much of our ill-fated relationship. But I'd been too busy to break up with her, too nice to put her out on the street with nowhere to go, too much of a gentleman to treat her the way she treated everyone else. I pulled my hand from hers. "Stop."

"Lennox, I'm sorry. I messed up."

"Messed up?" I said, fighting to control my temper. *Messing up* would be putting sugar in a big pot of spaghetti. *Messing up* was turning down the wrong street on the drive home. *Messing up* could even be choosing grilled salmon over fried catfish. Messing up didn't involve committing crimes, perpetrating fraud, and stealing money. Two things I hated—a thief and a con. Ayana was both.

"Yes," she pleaded. "I made a mistake."

I let out a humorless chuckle. "This is some bullshit," I muttered. "Go home, Yana."

Dana chimed in, "I'd like to know where the hell she got the money for that ring." My older sister had introduced me to Ayana years ago, and had apologized every day since for bringing the drama into my life. "She sure as

30

hell was crying broke a week ago when she had the nerve to ask me for fifty dollars."

"Who's to say she paid for the ring?" Emerie added with a shrug. "She's a fuckin' thief. I told you to turn her ass in to the police, Len."

"You need to leave," I told Ayana. "You've already embarrassed yourself—and me."

Ayana let out a loud, dramatic wail, covering her face. "I can't believe you're telling me no. After all we've been through together."

Dana stood then. "You played yourself, Ayana," she snapped. "Get the hell out of here. Lennox won't hit you, but I have no problem kicking your ass out of this restaurant."

Someone snorted. I didn't bother trying to figure out which bystander had done it. I didn't even care at that point. I just wanted this entire scene to end. Picking up the ring, I placed it in Yana's hand. "Don't try this again," I warned.

With shaky hands, Ayana stuffed the ring in her pocket. "I won't give up on us."

"I don't care what you do," I said. "Just do it far away from me and my family."

"Fine, I'm leaving. We'll talk later."

Shaking my head, I told her, "No, we won't."

After a few more minutes of her acting like the wounded victim by making eye contact with the older women and sniffing into a tattered piece of tissue another stranger had given her, Ayana finally walked out of the restaurant. And, again, all eyes were on me.

I dropped sixty dollars on the table. "Let's get out of here," I grumbled through clenched teeth.

Several minutes later, we sat down in a corner booth at another restaurant.

"How did she even know we were there?" Emerie asked, pouring cream into her coffee mug. "Does she have a tracker on your phone?"

Shrugging, I said, "She probably asked my teaching assistant. I don't know. It's not like I don't eat at Afternoon Delight at least once a week."

Vaughn took a sip from his mug. "Maybe it's time to change the routine a little, bruh."

"Or get a restraining order," Dana suggested. "Like I told you to do in the first place. It's not too late."

"I'm not doing that shit," I murmured. "I already have one against that student I told y'all about."

"Oh, yeah," Emerie said. "You never did finish telling us the story."

I'd just started telling my family about Dory Jensen when Ayana had shown up and dropped down on one knee to propose. Although it hadn't been a welcome proposal, it'd successfully taken my mind off the recent drama I had at the university.

Becoming the youngest associate professor for the Department of Afroamerican and African Studies at the University of Michigan was no small feat. I'd spent years focused on my end game, earning my Ph.D. earlier than anyone expected and becoming a published scholar before the age of thirty. Three degrees in less than ten years, countless articles in journals, numerous public lectures, and years of experience as a teaching assistant had made me the standout candidate. I'd missed family weddings, funerals, vacations, relationships, and life. But *one* student had nearly ruined everything I'd worked so hard to attain.

"I thought it was a little weird," I said, picking up my story where I'd left off earlier. "She'd hang around the classroom after lecture, visit office hours every week. I declined several invitations to go out for coffee or to dinner."

Emerie's mouth fell open. "What the hell?"

"Girl, it's gets worse," Dana said.

"I tried to be nice to her," I continued. "I treated her like everyone else in class, even though I was uncomfortable. Eventually, she started leaving gifts and writing notes. She even sent me naked pics of her. I reported the behavior to the chair, to my mentor, and to Dad." My father was partner at one of the biggest law firms in Ann Arbor. He'd given me invaluable advice on how to deal with her. "My colleagues brought her in for a meeting, gave her a warning, and threatened her with disciplinary action. Then, she showed up at my house and camped outside until I called the police on her. She finally left, but when I woke up the next morning, there was an old oil painting on my porch of a man and woman with afros looking up at the sky."

"Straight up?" Vaughn asked. "Why are you just now telling us this shit?"

"Because I thought I had it handled. Anyway, I started noticing strange behavior from the female students in my class—whispers, giggles, glares. Soon, I realized she'd told many of them that we had something going on. I even heard she'd shown pictures of someone's dick and told everyone it was me."

"That little bitch," Emerie whispered.

"It was a mess," I said. "The Department Chair moved her to another class taught by a friend of mine. But she showed up to my lecture like nothing had happened. I had to kick her out in front of everyone."

Dana drummed her fingers on the table. "So now he looks like the villain."

"Well, not to all of my students," I corrected. "A lot of

them see it for what it is. But I don't doubt her friends think I'm a piece of shit."

"Damn. All of that, and then you had to deal with Ayana's bullshit." Emerie placed her hand on top of mine and squeezed. "I'm so sorry, big brother. You can't seem to catch a break."

"It's those dimples," Dana said. "I always knew that smile would get him in trouble."

Chuckling, I bumped my big sister's shoulder. "Shut up."

"You might be on to something, sis," Emerie agreed. "He's probably in that classroom smiling and shit, dazzling those young girls with his intellect and his light brown eyes."

Vaughn barked out a laugh. "Some women are just unhinged."

I gave Vaughn a fist bump. "Exactly. *That* is not my fault."

Emerie gasped. "Wear a wedding ring."

"Shit," Vaughn murmured. "That won't work."

"Right?" Dana said. "That'll make him more attractive to those lil' heffas. Why don't you let me observe your class? I'll get those young girls right." She'd been threatening people since we were kids and claimed it was her official duty as the oldest.

"How about you observe *your* kids and *your* husband?" I suggested.

Rolling her eyes, she said, "Obviously you need my help. If you would've let me handle Ayana, we wouldn't have had to leave Afternoon Delight before I could get my buttery raisin toast today."

"I—" My phone buzzed in my pocket. Picking it up, I frowned at the notification that someone was at my front door. I opened up the app and immediately recognized the face in the camera. "Shit," I grumbled. "I need to go."

"Wait? What's going on?" Dana asked, concern in her eyes. "Is it Mom and Dad?"

I shook my head. "That student is at my house."

"I'm coming with you." Dana scooted out of the booth.

"Us too," Emerie said.

Shaking my head, I said, "No. I'll call Jace and we'll handle it."

"But—"

"Dana, the last thing I need is more drama. I'll call you when we get everything settled."

TWENTY MINUTES LATER, I pulled up at my house the same time my boy Jace, a Washtenaw County detective, did. "What's up?" I walked over to him. "Is she still here?"

Jace slid out of his car. "Yeah, and she's pretty belligerent, according to the officer."

On our way up the driveway, I scanned the front of my house. It didn't look like she'd broken any windows, but the door was wide open and…the woman holding my grandmother's vase was *not* Dory.

"That's not her," I murmured.

Jace looked up from his phone and muttered a curse before jogging over to the officer as he was handcuffing the woman who'd broken into my house. I followed him. "Blake, what the hell are you doing here?" he said.

She glanced at us, and her shoulders fell on a sigh. "Thank you! Jace, tell this man to take these damn cuffs off. Everything is a mistake."

"I'm not doing that," the young officer said. "You're under arrest."

35

"You can't arrest me because your wife left your sorry ass."

"I'm arresting you because you committed a crime, ma'am," the officer argued. "And I caught you holding his property."

She appealed to Jace again. "He's biased. He already told me my article contributed to the deterioration of his marriage."

"What article?" Jace asked.

"'It's Not Me, It's You,'" the officer grumbled.

"See, I told you," Blake said. "He can't be fair. Uncuff me."

"You broke into a house!" Jace yelled. "Why?"

Blake met my gaze, then tilted her head my way. "Him. *He's* why."

I should've been pissed, but for some strange reason I couldn't be mad. Chances were she didn't even remember me, but I definitely knew her. And just like the first time I'd met her, I couldn't help but be amused *and* intrigued by her.

Jace groaned. "Lennox Cole is the—"

"*Professor* Cole is the man who slept with his student, kicked her out of his class, then kept her shit from her."

In a few short months, Dory had damaged my reputation in ways I'd never dreamed possible until now. She'd managed to convince Blake that I was a piece of shit. Granted, our first meeting must've been pretty forgettable, since she didn't recognize me. But still…it didn't sit right with me. "That's not what happened," I said.

Her eyes locked on mine. "How did she know about the vase if she'd never been to your house?"

"I talked about it in one of my classes," I told her.

"Why should I believe you?" she asked.

"Why did you believe her?" I retorted, my voice low.

After a moment passed with no response from her, Jace said, "You're in trouble here, Blake."

She shrugged. "Well, get me out of it, Jace. Isn't that what you do?"

Curious, I wondered about the relationship between the two of them. Obviously, she was comfortable with him. But were they just friends? Or more than friends?

"Just answer the damn question," Jace snapped. "What are you doing here?"

"I was helping a client get her shit back," Blake said, matter-of-factly. "You know I wouldn't do anything crazy like this without a good reason. I'm not a thief."

Now *that* I believed. From the little conversation we'd had—while she'd been pretty drunk and distracted—she'd struck me as an honest, direct woman.

"I didn't think I was breaking into his house. She had a damn key," Blake said. "I didn't climb in a window, I walked through the front door."

Jace looked at me. "How does she have a key?"

"Last week, I misplaced my keys," I explained. "I couldn't find them in my office or my classroom. Eventually, my admin found them under her chair. Dory could've stolen them and made a copy."

"Very convenient," Blake said. "Besides, Jace, he's the one you need to be talking to. He gets off on sleeping with his students and taking their priceless belongings."

"Did Dory Jensen tell you this?" Jace asked. "She's been harassing Lennox for months. The judge granted a restraining order last week."

Blake froze. My guess? She was going over everything Dory had told her about me. Her shoulders sagged and she grumbled something incoherent.

Jace sighed. "Len, I believe her. She's not a liar. We've

been friends since we were kids. We lived on the same block for years."

"He has a crush on my twin sister," Blake added.

"Blake, shut up," Jace ordered.

Ignoring the warning, she continued, "I saved him from the switch time and again. Shit, his grandmother was tough. And I taught him how to do a foot sweep to beat up stupid Shamar Bolton."

"Shut up," Jace growled, rubbing the side of his face with his palm. "Let me handle this."

The officer scribbled something on his pad. "Blake… what's your last name again?"

"Young," I said. Two pairs of eyes met mine. "Her name is Blake Young."

Jace frowned. "You know her?"

Blake shot me a sidelong glance. "You know me?"

I narrowed my eyes on her. "Yes, I know who you are."

"Young," the officer murmured to himself as he continued to write on his small pad of paper. "Okay, city of residence?"

Blake cursed. "You'd already know this information if you wouldn't have been such a wea—"

Jace shushed her. "Be quiet. Officer Perry, can I have a word?"

The two of them walked toward the police cruiser, leaving me alone with Blake. She was watching me when I peered over at her again.

"What?" she asked.

"*You're* staring at *me*."

She rolled her eyes. "Because you keep looking at me. And how do you know my name?"

I hunched a shoulder. "Does it matter?"

"Actually, yes. As you can see, I'm not very popular with men who used to have wives or girlfriends who've read my work or heard me speak. So, yes, it matters. Especially if it colors your view of me."

"You're worried about my view of you?" I raised a brow. "After you broke into my house on the word of the woman who almost destroyed my career?"

"Well, when you say it like that...*damn.*"

"You're a therapist. How would you advise a client to handle this?"

"That's easy. I'd tell her to show mercy," she said with a shrug.

"I find that hard to believe."

"Well, how about fuck you?"

I smirked. "That sounds about right. Tell me something?"

"I'm not telling you shit—not until you tell me how you know me."

Folding my arms over my chest, I repeated my earlier question. "Why did you believe Dory?"

"Because. I'm sure your fine ass enjoys the kee-kee'ing from the young ladies in your classroom. Impressionable, vulnerable students who are there to learn African Studies, not get dick pics and asked out for coffee dates."

I wasn't sure which was worse—the fact that she'd almost stolen something valuable to me or the fact that she thought I'd send a picture of my dick to a student. Both felt like slaps in the face. "Do you always believe everything your clients tell you?"

"No," she admitted.

"What was so compelling about Dory's story that you broke into my house and stole my shit?"

Blake bit down on her bottom lip. "Listen, she was referred to me by someone I trust. She told me her story, and I thought you were a disgusting piece of shit."

"And now?"

Sighing, she said, "I trust Jace. Obviously, I got it wrong. I'm not a thief and I'm not a liar. You wanted me to tell you why I did it…that's why."

"Thanks for being honest."

"Are you going to tell me how you know me?"

"No." I smirked when she muttered a curse. "Maybe another time."

Blake apologized. "I can imagine how weird this shit is for you. Especially since I have a feeling everything Dory accused you of was something she'd done to you."

"Very perceptive."

"I'm sorry," she whispered.

Dory had taken something from me that I couldn't get back. But I wouldn't punish Blake for doing what she thought was right.

Jace approached us. "Len, can we…?"

"Let her go." I cleared my throat, keeping eye contact with Blake. "I'm not pressing charges."

Chapter 3

WHERE DID IT GO WRONG?

Blake

"*S*hould we wake her up?"

"No. Let her ass sleep. She's getting on my damn nerves anyway. Kicking me out like I'm a stranger."

I didn't dare move. Maybe they'd leave if I stayed still and kept my eyes closed. Yesterday had been a nightmare. I needed this reprieve, the quiet and solace of alone time with nobody but my bed and my television.

"She's going to be mad she didn't get some of this breakfast I brought. Those pancakes are good as hell."

Hot, buttery pancakes sounded so good. Knowing Dexter, he'd ordered the bacon extra crispy and the eggs scrambled hard with cheese. *Yum.*

"I feel so bad. It's my fault she got arrested."

Aw. My poor niece was blaming herself. Maybe I should put her out of her misery and open my eyes? *Yeah, no.*

"It's not your fault, baby girl. It's *her* fault for believing your crazy-ass friend. We all knew there was something wrong with her the first time you brought her around."

It was just like Dallas to point out how stupid I was without even saying the word. *I hate her.*

"But if it wasn't for me, she wouldn't have even talked to her," Raven said.

"Again, this is on Blake. She knew better. I keep telling her to check that temper."

"Says the woman who threatens to cut a bitch every chance she gets."

Thank you, Asa!

"Not a bitch, a muthafucka," Dallas corrected. "And it's just an expression. I'm not about that jail life. I just talk a good game."

"I think I'm getting ready to have this baby." Bliss groaned, and I was almost tempted to open my eyes to see if she was okay. Almost. "I feel all this pressure in my pelvic area."

"Shit, why are you talking about your pelvic area?"

Dallas snorted. "Stop acting like you don't know about women's pelvic areas, Asa. All those women up in the gym offering you a taste."

"Ew. That is so nasty, Uncle Asa."

"Those women aren't my sister," my little brother said.

"Did Jace tell you anything else, Dexter?"

"Not much. Just that his guy refused to press charges."

That *guy* had haunted my dreams. I'd thought about where Lennox Cole could've met me all damn day. So far, I'd ruled out sex, certain I would've remembered fucking his fine ass. That left work, a client's ex, school... I was perplexed. And so curious. Oh, and embarrassed too.

"Did they find Dory?" Dallas asked. I pictured her

peering at Dexter with her arms crossed and a stern lawyerly look on her face.

"No," Dex replied. "Raven, have you seen her?"

"She disappeared, took all her shit out of her dorm room."

As far as I was concerned, that girl better have left town. Because if I laid eyes on her again, I'd be tempted to lay her out.

"Ooh, you cussed," Asa teased. "I'm telling your dad."

Raven giggled. "So. I'm grown."

"I might need to go to the hospital," Bliss said. "I'm probably in labor."

"Let's wake her up."

"Fuck that, Dallas," Duke said with a groan. "And take your ass over there and sit on that ball, Bliss. Practice your breathing. Blake just needs sleep—or a good fuck."

Or a good fight. I was still pissed about my damn juice. So pissed I wanted to kick him in his shin.

"I'm kind of worried about her," Dex said. I felt the weight of someone sitting on my mattress. "She didn't even eat dinner last night."

"Shit, have you seen her lately? She punched me yesterday morning."

I heard a soft thump and a whoosh. *What the hell are they doing?*

"Because you ate all of her food and drank her favorite juice, fool," Bliss pointed out. "And I'm not bouncing on that damn ball."

"I think someone needs to call Granny. This is pretty bad. She's been in here for hours."

No.

"Hell no," Dex said. "Mom doesn't need to be here for this. She's busy enough getting ready for that baby shower."

"What about Granddad?" Raven asked. "Should we tell him?"

"That would be a double hell nah," Duke muttered. "We got this, bubble gum. No parents needed."

"I'm calling my dad."

No!

"If you pick up that phone and call Tristan's fun-killin' ass," Duke warned, "I will—"

"Fuck it, I'm waking her up," Dallas announced.

And I'd officially had it. "I'm up!" I shouted, opening my eyes. I peered at the faces of many of my siblings and my niece staring at me like I was lab specimen. Grabbing a pillow, I smacked Duke upside the head. "Get out of my room."

"Shit," he grunted, recovering fast and bopping me in my face. "You gone stopping hitting me, B. I told y'all to leave her grumpy ass alone."

Sitting up, I glanced at each of them. "You told them right."

Dallas sat down on the bed. "We have that wedding today. We RSVP'd, and we can't miss it."

I fell back on the mattress and rolled over, pulling my comforter over my head. "I'm not going to that shit. I'm staying home."

"Getcho ass out of the damn bed." Dex tugged on my blanket.

Duke thumped me, and I smacked his hand. "Stop," I hissed.

"That's what you get, punk," he said. "Get ready. We need to be at the church in an hour."

I jumped out of the bed and walked to my bedroom door. "Okay, that's it. Leave me the hell alone. I'm not going to that damn wedding."

My siblings filed out of my room, too slowly for my

taste. Raven stayed behind. I squeezed her chin. "It's not your fault, baby. Dallas was right. This is on me."

My niece shot me a sad smile. "Okay, but I'm sorry."

"Don't apologize anymore. Now, go on. Send my condolences to the happy couple."

"Don't you mean well wishes?" Raven asked innocently.

I shrugged. "I meant what I said." I waved at her and closed my door.

Attending the wedding of an ex was not my idea of a good time. The moment I'd received the invitation for Aiden's wedding to the new love of his life, I'd tossed it in the trash. It was only after the monumental guilt trip my mother had lain on me that I'd agreed to go.

Strangely, Aiden was the only man who'd been my "boyfriend" twice. Our first relationship had lasted just long enough for me to know he wasn't the one. And I damn sure wasn't the girl for him. The reason I knew that was because I'd cheated on him after one day. Granted, we'd been in the sixth grade, but still...I couldn't pass up Sour Patch Kids and Faygo Red Pop. Franklin Bell had all the goodies, so I'd agreed to go with him instead of Aiden. Which made Sunday School pretty awkward.

During college, Aiden had asked me out again. For some reason, I couldn't tell him no. I'd cared about him; I'd loved him. He'd been a bit of a nerd, a bad dresser, a terrible kisser, and very deliberately celibate; but he was respectful, nice-looking...an overall good guy. *Too good for me.*

Despite my best intentions, I'd hurt him. While some part of me had wanted it to work, I'd known it wouldn't last. He'd wanted a virtuous woman, and I wasn't it. I was young, full of myself, and determined to make my own rules for my life. In the end, I'd been bored with him and couldn't force myself to stay, no matter how much I'd cared.

Breaking up with him was the hardest thing I'd had to do—so hard that I'd cried when it was over. And I didn't shed tears lightly. The worst part? Losing the friendship we'd built since childhood. For years, he'd hated to see me coming, which was why I'd avoided him at all costs. Not because I was scared, but because I didn't want to hurt him anymore. In the end, though, he'd become the man I always thought he'd be. Gentle, kind, handsome, and giving. All the things I hadn't wanted back then. All the things I didn't think I wanted now.

A knock on the door pulled me from my reverie. Bliss poked her head in. "Sissy, Mom called. She said you're going to the wedding."

Rolling my eyes, I told her, "Fine. Give me half an hour."

THE WEDDING STARTED ON TIME. Dallas and I had barely made it before the processional. As a result, we had to sit toward the back of the church. Which was good, because I was too far away for my mother to send me death glares for being late. I glanced toward the front of the sanctuary at Aiden, standing with his head held high and a wide grin on his face. He looked good, happy.

The bridesmaids were escorted down the aisle to music I didn't recognize. Then, the bride appeared. Dressed in all white, with no skin showing whatsoever, she slowly walked toward her groom.

"She's pretty," Dallas whispered.

"Yeah," I murmured.

"That dress, though."

I snickered. "Tell me about it. I wonder why they pushed the wedding back?" The original wedding had been scheduled for last June, but they'd moved it to January. "It's cold as hell outside." *Oops.* I'd just cursed in church.

"Mom said it had something to do with honoring his grandmother by having the wedding on her birthday."

"Oh," I grumbled. My mood hadn't improved at all, even after the pancakes and bacon I'd scarfed down on the way to the church.

Dallas gave me sidelong glance. "What's wrong with you?"

Staring at Aiden, I sighed. "He looks so handsome."

"You're surprised?"

Shrugging, I said, "Yeah, actually. I molded him. I dressed him. *I* taught him how to be fine. None of that worked while I was with him, but I can see it's paying off nicely. Now that he's a rock star, he's giving all my hard work to some other chick." *Some other nice chick.* "This could've been my wedding." Dallas snorted, and I elbowed her. "Shut up."

"You broke up with *him*, Blake—for good reasons. You did the thing you tell so many women to do on a daily basis. You recognized something wasn't right, and no matter how you felt about him, you knew it was best to walk away."

I hated when Dallas was right, because she never let anyone live it down. "I know, but still…" I didn't even want Aiden anymore. I had no idea why I was feeling this way, why everything in my life seemed so out of place that I was ogling the groom I could've had but didn't want. "He's going to be a good husband, that's all," I added lamely.

Dallas pressed the back of her hand to my forehead.

"What have you done with my sister? What is with this life ennui?"

I let out a heavy sigh. "I should probably drink all the cognac tonight," I mused, ignoring her question. "It's been long enough." Some church mother shushed me, and I smiled at her. Once she turned around, I rolled my eyes. "Let's get out of here."

"We can't leave," Dallas said.

I scanned the crowd. I recognized a few faces, several I hadn't seen in years, some I didn't care to see again ever. On the left side of the church—the bride's side—I checked out several of the guests. Some of them looked familiar as well, but… "*Oh, shit.*"

Dallas pinched my knee, and the three older women in front of me turned around and glared at me.

Sinking in my seat, I murmured, "I said that out loud, didn't I?"

"Forgive her, Lord," Dallas whispered. "She's not herself today. And forgive *me*, Lord, for not sitting with my good sister, Bliss."

Embarrassed, I tried to focus on the ceremony. But I couldn't help but look over at the other side of the church again, locking eyes with a smirking Lennox. I swallowed, letting out a slow breath. Talk about fine as hell. Raven was right when she'd told me his professor pic didn't do him justice. Because that smile… *Damn*. If I hadn't been handcuffed when I saw him, I might've been tempted to do something about it. Like invite him over and end my drought. Oh, yes, I was definitely attracted to Mr. Cole. But there was something else too. The way he talked to me, the way he looked at me, the way he was. Fine, but not *just* fine. Smart, but not *just* smart. Sexy, but not *just* sexy. The whole package. *Or I could just be horny.*

I met his waiting gaze again and forced a smile. What

was he doing here? *Please don't let him be related to Aiden in any way.* That would be tragic. He was sitting on the bride's side, though, so…

Dallas raised a brow. "Are you okay?"

"That's him."

"Who?" She searched the sanctuary. "I don't see anyone."

"Lennox."

Frowning, she said, "Lennox?"

"Professor Cole," I whisper-yelled, once again drawing the ire of the women in front of me. *Sorry,* I mouthed. "Third row from the back, seated on the aisle," I told Dallas.

It took a few seconds, but I knew the exact moment my sister spotted Lennox, because she whispered, "Oh, damn." She cleared her throat. "Um… Fine danamug, Sissy. I might have to introduce myself."

I glared at her. "Don't even try it."

Dallas smirked. "Well, now. You're being quite territorial."

"We have rules, Sissy."

Dallas and I were the only Young ladies who weren't about that relationship life. She was my road dawg, and we traveled together often. And we were attracted to the same type of man, which was why we developed rules. The main one? The sister who'd seen the man first had dibs.

"Whatever," she grumbled. "You're on punishment."

I shifted in my seat. "Rules still apply."

"Don't let him go to waste, then."

A few more songs, a praise dance, heartfelt vows, and a chaste kiss later, the wedding was over. Aiden and his new bride jumped the broom and raced out of the church. I was grateful too. Because every time I'd glanced over at Lennox, he'd been looking at me with those light brown eyes and smiling with those deep dimples on display. And I was hot. *I need some air.*

We met the rest of my family in the church foyer. I hugged my mother, fidgeting under her stare for a moment before I asked, "Yes, Mom?"

She tilted her head, assessing me, seeing me. There was little to nothing I could ever get past Victoria Young. Her omniscient skillset had ruined many a plan growing up. My mom ran a finger over my cheek, like she'd done so many times. The tickle in my nose, signaling I might cry, startled me. "It's going to be okay, baby." Her soft voice soothed something deep inside me. Then, she wrapped her arms around me again. "I love you, sweetie."

I held on to her for dear life, praying the entire time that not nary a tear would fall. "Love you too," I whispered.

She pulled back eventually, smiling. "Let's talk soon. I miss you."

I nodded. "Okay."

Winking at me, she turned her attention to Bliss and her belly. Having eight kids in less than ten years must've been hard for my mom. But she'd mothered us with grace and understanding. Her and my father were present in all of our lives, giving freely and sowing into our lives in ways I'd forever be grateful for. I loved both of them dearly, and I didn't know what I'd do without them.

My dad pulled me into a hug. "My Blakey. You look beautiful."

"Thanks, Daddy," I said. "You like my new glasses?"

He grinned and shook his head. "Not really. I told you about those big frames. People wore that back in the Eighties."

Laughing, I kissed his cheek. "I knew I could count on you to make me rethink my whole ensemble." Dr. Stewart

Young couldn't lie to save his life. So we'd all grown used to the simple truth. Over the years, there had been many hurt feelings, but we were a lot stronger for it too.

An older man approached us and asked to speak to my father.

"Love you, babe," Dad said as he walked away with the man.

Duke inched closer to me. "Are you talking to me again?"

I eyed him. "I guess. You still have to leave, though."

"I'll see you tonight," he announced as if I hadn't told him he had to stay somewhere else.

Shaking my head, I leaned over to Dallas. "Why are we all standing here?" I asked. "Is there food or something?"

"Supposedly, there's an hors d'oeuvres reception here."

"Which means no liquor," Dexter grumbled.

Lennox walked out of the sanctuary at that moment. And I couldn't take my eyes off him as he greeted people with that grin of his. By the time he noticed me, I'd seen him charm the pants off several women, young and old. Yet, he made no move to approach me. Which was oddly disappointing.

A short while later, we were ushered into the reception hall, and I made a beeline to the dessert table. Our home church had some of the best bakers. The little cheesecake cups were my favorite, and I intended to get one before they were all gone.

Luckily, everyone else was standing in line for the bite-sized chicken nuggets and fruit bowls. I had my pick of desserts. Deciding on strawberry, I picked up the cup and a spoon and immediately sampled the delicious treat. Unable to help myself, I let out a groan.

"Good, huh?"

I froze, spoon in my mouth. Peering up, I smiled at

Lennox and nodded. He grabbed a blueberry cheesecake cup and tasted it. His groan went straight to my pussy, and I immediately felt dirty for being turned on in the house of the Lord. "I love these things," I offered.

He ate another spoonful. "I can see why."

My eyes were laser focused on his lips, but I managed to say, "They tell us to only take one, but I always eat two."

"I won't tell if you don't."

A moment passed while warring emotions threatened to knock me off my square. This definitely wasn't me. I knew how to talk to a man. This man should've been no different than any other guy. *Blake Muthafuckin' Young, get your shit together and stop acting like a smitten schoolgirl who doesn't know her way around a dick.* "I love these things," I said finally. "I have to stop myself from going overboard."

"Is this your church?"

I nodded. "My family have been members since we were kids."

"Friends of the groom?"

"Yep." I chuckled. "You could say that. Are you here for the bride?"

"Roxy is my best friend's little sister."

"Oh. Small world, huh?"

"Very." His lingering gaze made me uncomfortable in a good way. I liked his eyes on me. And I wondered how his hands would feel too.

"Professor Cole, I should probably apologize again about yesterday."

He shook his head. "No need."

"Seriously, thanks for not pressing charges."

"I believe you didn't know you were breaking into my place. This is all Dory's fault."

"Trust me, she won't be happy to see me when I track her down."

He snickered. "Hopefully, it won't take long."

"It won't. I have my ways." I'd already decided to ask Tristan, who owned a PI firm, to look into her past. "I'll find her."

Lennox handed me his business card. "Keep me posted."

I stared at it, brushing my thumb over his name. "Sure. Are you going to tell me how you know me?"

He smirked. "Maybe," he teased.

"Come on, man. Can you at least tell me if I was nice to you?"

Blessing me with a full smile, he nodded. "You were. A little drunk, but very nice."

I raised a brow. "Did I hit on you?"

"No."

I sighed. "Bummer."

Chuckling, he said, "You crack me up."

"As in laughing *with* me? Or *at* me?"

His gaze dropped to my mouth, and warmth spread through my body as if he'd kissed me. "With you. And if you'd hit on me, you'd remember."

A smile tugged at my lips. "Good to know."

"Sissy?"

I blinked, glancing over at the intruder—Bliss. "Hey," I whispered. "Are you okay?"

She eyed Lennox, shooting her best flirtatious smile up at him. "I'm good." She held out her hand. "Hi, I'm Bliss."

"Twins?" he asked.

We both said yes at the same time. Bliss laughed. "And best friends."

"Bliss, this is Professor Cole."

"Lennox," he corrected.

My twin's eyes widened and her mouth fell open. "Oh,

wow. Hey."

"Good to meet you," he told her. "But I see you already know who I am."

"Um, yeah. Oh, well…" Bliss stammered. "Thanks for not pressing charges against my sister. She really didn't mean it."

He nodded, never taking his eyes off me. "I know."

"She's really sorry," she explained unnecessarily.

"Bliss," I warned.

"Really sorry," my twin repeated.

"He already knows," I told her.

"Anyway, I just came here to let you know we're heading back to the big house," Bliss announced, "to have dinner together."

"Okay." I finished my cheesecake. "I'll be right there."

"We'll be upstairs." Bliss winked at me, said her good-byes to Lennox, then waddled off.

Shrugging, I said, "I'd better go. Maybe next time I see you, you'll tell me more?"

"Definitely. Call me if you hear anything about Dory."

"I will."

"Bye, Blake Young."

I grinned. "Bye, Lennox Cole." I started to walk away, then I remembered something. Turning back, I picked up another cup of dessert. "Have to have two."

Laughing, he grabbed another cup. "Like I said, I won't tell if you don't."

Chapter 4

SOMETHING IN THE PAST

Lennox

*I*t had been a week since Ayana had embarrassed the hell out of both of us, and I'd finally decided to venture into Afternoon Delight to meet my colleague and friend, Lincoln Wilson, Jr, for breakfast. The hostess recognized me immediately, throwing a bit of shade at the entire scene with my ex before she slid me her phone number and told me to call her.

The regular waitress had simply welcomed me back, then showed me to my booth. I'd just ordered when Linc walked into the café.

"What's up, bruh?" He gave me dap and slid into the booth. "Sorry I'm late, man. I had to dig my shit out of a ditch this morning."

Snow was part of Michigan's charm. Or at least that's what I told myself every time we got more than five inches. Last night was tame compared to the blizzard that had ruined Thanksgiving last year. But the drop in temperatures had made the roads slick and dangerous. Luckily, I only had a ten-minute drive to campus. But Linc lived at least forty miles away, so his commute was a beast.

"Damn, bruh." I sipped my coffee. "But don't you think you should finally trade in that old-ass car for a SUV or something?"

Linc placed his order with the waitress. When she walked away, he said, "I've already made an appointment to check out that new Bronco. I'm sick of this shit."

"Makes you want to take that job offer, huh?"

Last month, Linc had received an offer to join the faculty at Howard University, and had been strongly considering the move. Rubbing the back of his head, he nodded. "It's been on my mind. My parents keep trying to talk me out of it, claiming they'd miss us."

"You don't believe them?"

He waved a dismissive hand my way. "Nah, they just want the kids to stay here." He laughed. "I called my mother on it, and all she could do was smile."

"How is Ms. Layla?" Linc's mother was my sixth-grade teacher. After I left her class, she'd stayed in touch, always checking on me, even after I'd graduated from high school and college. "Is she still regretting retirement?"

Linc nodded. "She's ready to go back in the classroom, but my father is keeping her busy. They've been traveling all over the place."

"That's cool."

He eyed me. "I heard the situation with that student blew up."

I wasn't surprised he'd heard about Dory. While Linc worked for the Department of Political Science, our departments worked very close together, and people talked.

Seemed like everyone loved to gossip, especially faculty. "What did you hear exactly?"

Shrugging, he said, "Man, you know by the time I heard anything, the story was somewhere left of the truth. I was told she broke into your office and stole a painting."

I chuckled, shaking my head. "Bullshit. She didn't break into my office. She left a painting on my porch, *then* broke into my house."

He leaned back in his chair. "What the fuck is wrong with her?"

"Hell if I know." The waitress set our food down on the table and disappeared. "She ran away when the police showed up, and no one has heard from her since."

"Damn, bruh. Did she get away with anything valuable?"

"Nah, but she had an accomplice."

He cut into his short stack of pancakes. "Another student?" he asked with a raised brow.

"Actually it was your cousin Blake."

Pausing, fork midair, he said, "Wait a minute…Blake broke into your house?"

"Yeah," I answered.

Linc pushed his plate away. "Hell no."

"I'm serious."

"Shit. How did you find out?"

"The police caught her—with my grandmother's vase in her hands."

"Shut the hell up. They arrested her?"

I shook my head. "I didn't press charges."

"This is crazy, bruh. Did she recognize you?"

I laughed. "Nah, man. Dory lied to her, told her this sob story about me keeping her shit at my house. Blake thought she was helping Dory get her belongings."

Linc stared ahead, his eyes wide. "Now, that's hard to believe. Did you tell her who you were?"

"Not yet." I smirked, recalling our last interaction at Roxy's wedding. Of all the people I'd expected to run into at the church, she hadn't been one of them. But once I'd seen her, she was all I could see. There was something about her that had me transfixed, from her smile to the way she moved, the way she handled herself. She was refreshing, genuine. It'd been a while since I could laugh with a woman who wasn't my sister. I hadn't realized how much I missed that until now. I probably should've told her who I was, but I enjoyed teasing her.

"Didn't y'all sit at the same table at the reception?"

Four years ago, Blake and I had ended up seated next to each other at Linc's wedding reception. She'd arrived late and couldn't sit with her siblings, who'd taken up the entire table next to ours. We hadn't had a real conversation that night, nor any of the other times I'd seen her at random events. But she'd definitely left an impression.

"We did," I confirmed. "But I was with Ayana, so…" My ex had a nasty attitude, especially in public around other women. She'd always acted entitled to all of my attention, which in turn made women avoid me. Even if I'd known them for years. We'd argued about it countless times over the course of the relationship.

"Oh, yeah…" he said. "She even treated Courtney like shit."

"Don't remind me," I grumbled. Linc's older sister, Courtney, had gone out of her way to be friendly to Ayana when we'd run into them at a restaurant. But Ayana's cold demeanor had made it impossible. That had been the beginning of the end for us.

"Now that I think of it—" Linc chuckled, "—Blake was pretty drunk the night of my wedding."

"I remember," I said.

"We partied long and hard," he added.

"How are y'all related again?" All I'd known was they were cousins. Linc didn't talk too much about his family. I sensed it was because there was a lot of trauma there. I knew his father had struggled with addiction in the past, and had worked hard to leave that life behind. I didn't know much beyond that.

"My father and Blake's mother are cousins. They grew up more like siblings, though—lived in the same house. Aunt Vicky is the only family member my father maintained contact with after my grandmother died."

"So you're close?"

"I'm close to Paityn, Blake's older sister. We're around the same age. Courtney is close to their oldest brother, Tristan."

I nodded, my mind running with questions I wouldn't ask. Suddenly, I wanted to know everything about Blake— where she'd gone to school, how she'd chosen her career, what she liked to do when she wasn't counseling her clients. Did she have a man? Did she *want* one?

"I can't believe you didn't know her," Linc said. "Y'all are the same age. She went to Pioneer. You had to have seen her at football games or something, even though y'all went to rival high schools."

Pioneer High School was in Ann Arbor. While I'd grown up in the neighboring city, Ypsilanti, it felt like our hometowns we were worlds apart. "That doesn't matter. I didn't even know everyone in *my* graduating class. I was too busy playing ball, trying not to get in trouble, and working."

Linc sprinkled salt and pepper over his eggs. "Shit, I get that. I am surprised Blake would break into your house on the word of a student, though," he mused. "She's a fighter, but she's not reckless. Well…" He sucked in a deep breath. "Not really."

Resting my elbows on the table, I asked, "What do you mean by that?"

He hunched a shoulder. "She had a lot of energy. It often got her in trouble. But nothing like this."

"She told me Dory was referred to her by someone she trusted," I explained. "She did apologize, though."

Frowning, Linc said, "Well, I'm definitely going to ask some questions. Thanks for not sending my cousin to jail, bruh."

We finished our breakfast, shooting the shit about work and home. The more Linc talked, the more I knew he was D.C. bound. His wife was from Virginia and had been wanting to move closer to her family for a while. Linc had been complaining about the weather for as long as I'd known him. I definitely wouldn't be shocked if he announced his departure soon.

After breakfast, I spent the rest of my morning in class. The talk had died down some, and several female students had approached me to apologize for believing the rumors. That afternoon, I caught up on work, attended a faculty meeting, and made it out of the building on time for once. Instead of going home, I headed to the bar.

The Ice Box was packed when I got there. Friday nights had become a popular night at the hometown bar, but I knew one of the owners so I was able to reserve a pool table.

Jace arrived a few minutes later. "What's up, man?" He ordered a drink while I racked up the balls. "How long you been here?"

"Not long." I bent low, aimed, and took my shot. Examining the table, I decided my strategy and set up my next shot. "I didn't order food yet, though."

"I'm not hungry." He nodded at the waitress who'd dropped his beer off. "Ate at the station."

"Alright."

"Got an update on Dory today."

I shifted my attention from the table to him. "Did you find her?"

Shaking his head, he said, "Not yet, but I'm working with Blake's brother on this. We found out some things that might surprise you." Nothing Dory did would've surprised me at that point, but I told him to continue. "After talking to her mother, we discovered she'd lied about her background."

Standing to my full height, I asked, "I thought her mother was dead?" During office hours one day, Dory had shared that she'd lost both of her parents in a car accident.

"No. Her mother is very much alive and living in Grand Rapids."

I took a long gulp of beer. "Why would she lie about that?"

"Who knows. For sympathy?"

"What else?"

"Her mother didn't even know she'd enrolled in school. She thought Dory had moved to Texas. I guess Dory would call her mother every Sunday and act like she was in Houston, talk about job she didn't have, send pictures of an apartment that wasn't hers."

"Wait, that doesn't even make any sense." Although Dory was technically an adult, I couldn't imagine a parent not knowing where their college-aged kid was living. My parents had been a huge presence throughout my entire life, and my mother hadn't thought twice about surprising my ass on campus. Even when I'd pleaded with her to call first.

"As a minor, she got into some trouble with the law.

Her juvenile records are sealed, but her mother explained she'd gotten violent with a high school classmate—over a teacher."

This keeps getting better. "So I'm not the first, huh?"

He shook his head. "Nah, man. You're not even the second. Before she came to the University, she attended a community college in Kalamazoo. A professor there had filed a complaint against her and later dropped it."

"Why did he drop the charges?"

"Because he was a piece of shit. They had an affair for three months before she moved here. Apparently, she saw a video of you giving a lecture and decided she wanted to be Mrs. Lennox Cole."

"Whatever, man," I grumbled. "What the hell am I supposed to do with this? She knows where I live, where I work."

"We have reason to believe she's still in town. We'll find her. She'll slip up at some point."

"In the meantime, I just...what? Lay low?"

"I'm not saying that. Just be careful. No telling what her state of mind is."

As angry as I was at the situation, I hoped Dory got the help she needed. Obviously, she'd been spiraling out of control for quite some time. At the same time, I needed her to get help far away from me. I let out a heavy sigh. "I guess. I already changed my locks. The security company is coming to install more cameras tomorrow morning."

"That works." Jace frowned, grumbling a curse.

Turning my head to see who he was muggin', I noticed that a group of men had gathered near the bar. I didn't recognize any of them, but Jace obviously had. "You good?"

"Shit," he mumbled.

Out of the corner of my eye, I spotted Blake stalking

toward the rowdy group. She was laser focused on one in particular and stopped right in front of him.

Jace sighed, setting his beer down. "I need to go handle this."

Before I could ask any questions, Jace approached the crowd. And before I could question myself, I inched toward the group.

"Can I talk to you?" Blake asked.

The guy snorted. "What do you want?" he slurred.

She motioned with her head. "Alone?"

"Alone, huh?" The guy gave another man a high five.

Blake smiled, but it didn't reach her eyes, giving me a clue that something was very wrong. "Yes."

The man seemed to sense the same thing, because he said, "Nah, Blake. I'm good. You can say what you need to say right here."

Shrugging, she said, "Sure?"

"Very."

She beckoned him closer with her forefinger. "Did you hit my sister?" One of the guys next to him stood, like he was going to do something to her. When Jace stepped forward, Blake placed her hand against his chest. "I got this, Jace."

Scanning the immediate area, I noticed the stares from several people and a few cellphones out, probably ready to record. I rolled my sleeves up, ready to jump in if I had to, because I had no tolerance for any man who hit a woman.

"Tyler?" Blake continued, her voice soft, measured. "I'm going to ask you again. Did you hit my very pregnant sister?"

Tyler glanced back at his boys, then to Jace, then to Blake. "Did your sister tell you that?" Blake didn't respond; she didn't even blink. "Man, get out of here. I don't have time for your bullshit." He shoved her.

Seconds later, Tyler was on the ground, and Blake was kicking the shit out of him. Jace grabbed her, but she kicked herself free from his hold too. Before she could reach Tyler again, I jumped into action, snaking an arm around her waist and pulling her away.

"Fuck you, muthafucka!" she shouted at Tyler, bucking against my hold. "Don't you ever lay your punk-ass hands on my sister again."

Tyler groaned. "Call the police," he stammered, trying to stand. He fell back on the floor. "Your ass is going to jail for assault, Blake."

Jace leaned down and grumbled, "As far as I'm concerned, it was self-defense. Everybody in here saw you push her first. One more thing…the next time you think about putting your hands on Bliss or Blake, don't. It would give me nothing but pure pleasure to lock your sorry ass up."

As far as *I* was concerned, Tyler got what he deserved. And it made me more intrigued about the woman who'd given it to him.

Chapter 5

YOU OUGHTA KNOW

Blake

I *blacked out.*

The rage I felt, the anger threatening to split me open, had barely subsided, but my surroundings started coming into focus. The crowd, the stares, the flashes of light from camera phones, Tyler writhing in pain on the floor.

Sounds registered next. The crunch of glass beneath my feet, laughter behind me, whispers beside me, the sports commentator on the televisions, and the raspy voice against my ear. Suddenly, I felt arms around me—strong, steady—and realized someone was holding on to me, talking to me.

Jace stood off to my side, talking on the phone. *It's not him.* I bucked against the person, determined to free myself. All the tricks I'd learned, all the maneuvers that had served me well in the past…nothing worked.

The forceful command I'd intended to growl out turned into a lame and weary, "Let me go."

"You're okay," the voice whispered. "I got you."

I gave up the fight, sagging against the hard chest at my back. "Fuck you," I spit out. The soft chuckle in my ear soothed me for some reason, put me at ease a little. "I'm good," I breathed. "I'm calm."

A moment later, I felt the hold on me wane and I was able to tear myself free. Whirling around, I was ready to clock the jerk. "Don't fuckin'…" *Touch me again, muthafucka* died on my lips when I realized the man who'd held me until my breathing had steadied, the man who'd tried his best to keep me from putting Tyler in the hospital, was Lennox.

He reached out, but I backed away, nearly tripping over a bar stool that had tipped over. Lennox acted quickly, pulling me back toward him so I didn't hit the floor. His tight grip held me against him, only this time we were chest to chest, eyes on each other.

Swallowing, I let out a slow breath. "You."

That damn smirk formed on his perfect lips. "You," he repeated.

I licked my lips and stepped away from him. This time, he let me go. "I—" Two police officers entered the bar. "I fucked up," I whispered.

One of the officers helped Tyler up, while the other one pulled out handcuffs. *My ass is really going to jail.* Yet, the officer didn't even look at me. Instead, he calmly placed the cuffs on Tyler and escorted him out of the bar.

Lennox leaned down, pressed his lips against my ear. "He pushed you first. You defended yourself."

The details were a hazy. Bliss' confession, her loud sobs, her contractions, my feeling of hopelessness… I remembered driving toward my parents' house when I spotted Tyler's car in the parking lot. I remembered walking into the bar and seeing that nigga laughing with his friends, acting like he hadn't put his hands on my sister. But everything else seemed jumbled.

I peered up at Lennox. "Really?" My voice sounded foreign to my own ears.

He searched my eyes, but there was something about his stare. I felt seen, almost like he understood me. "Yes."

"I didn't...?"

He shook his head. "You didn't," he confirmed.

The lump that had formed in my throat felt big, too big to swallow. I wanted to say something but couldn't find the right words. I couldn't articulate how grateful I was in that moment.

"Blake," Jace said, approaching us. "You can go home."

With wide eyes, I glanced at Jace. "Are you sure?" My eyes burned with unshed tears. I wouldn't let them fall.

Jace shot me a sad smile. "You can give a statement tomorrow." He pulled me into a warm embrace. "I'll check on you later." He kissed my brow. "Tell Bliss...I'm sorry." Then, he walked out of the bar.

"I have to go," I whispered to no one in particular.

Lennox squeezed my hand. "Not like this. Come on."

Several minutes later, I was seated across from Lennox at a nearby café. We hadn't spoken since we'd arrived. He merely deposited me at a booth, went to grab two cups of coffee, and returned with cream, sugar, honey, milk— everything a person might need to make a decent cup.

My mind wouldn't stop running. I couldn't get the image of Bliss out of my head; I couldn't stop hearing her cry. I needed to go to her, but I also couldn't move.

"Did you call your sister?" Lennox asked, pulling me from my thoughts.

Clearing my throat, I shook my head. "I'm going to text my other sister. She's there with her. I just needed a moment." I would've never left Bliss alone, no matter how angry I was. Dallas had arrived shortly before I'd left. I hadn't told her anything—I'd just walked out.

Did Bliss tell her what happened with Tyler? If she had, all of my siblings and my parents were probably at my house right this minute. Luckily, Tyler had been arrested. I imagined my brothers would be trying to find him and wear his ass out. Duke especially.

"Bliss is the good one," I said, my voice small. "She's so sweet, giving, loving. He used her from the beginning." I met Lennox's gaze, noted the concern in his brown eyes. "I protected her. I tried…" I squeezed my eyes closed. "I wasn't there. I've been so angry, so distant. She'd been calling all day, but I stayed away from my house because I needed time to myself. I needed a *me* day."

We'd had a busy week. Several family members and friends had traveled to Michigan for Bliss' baby shower last Saturday, so there was always a dinner, always a game night, always something to attend. Today was the first day I didn't have to do family stuff. So I'd spent the day at the spa by myself. Instead of going home afterward, I'd gone to the movies, grabbed a bite to eat alone. Finally, I'd made it home, only to find my sister on the floor, bawling her eyes out. It had taken her a while to talk to me, but when she had, I couldn't control my rage. Not just at Tyler, but at myself for being such a moody bitch. I'd made the decision to go on this Yak-less, dick-less journey. None of my family deserved the wrath I'd unleashed on them this past week. Now, all I felt was guilt. Because I could've been there.

"It's not your fault," Lennox said, placing his hand on mine.

Warmth spread from my hand up my arm and filled

every space of my body. The simple touch, the innocent gesture, was more than him comforting me. For some reason, I couldn't help but feel safe with him, almost like I could share anything. Which was ridiculous, since I barely knew him. I'd only seen him two other times that I could remember, and one of those times I'd been caught breaking into his house. He should've hated me. Hell, I would've hated his ass if the shoe was on the other foot, if he'd accused me of doing something damning. But he'd shown me grace under extraordinary circumstances.

"As much as we want to be the savior, as much as we want to fix it, sometimes we can't be there," he continued. "That doesn't make you a bad person, it makes you human."

I stared at him. His words...the intensity in his eyes told me he'd been there. I wanted to know more about it, more about him. "I didn't expect to end up at that bar," I confessed.

"We never do." He smirked. "Sometimes the bar is where we need to be, though. Drinks, food...a good bar fight. Sounds like fun to me."

I laughed. "Thank you."

He sipped his coffee, eyeing me over the rim of his cup. "Glad I could make you laugh."

I picked up my phone. Dallas had sent five texts, each one worse than the other. Not with bad news, but with her cussing my ass out for not responding. I fired off a text: *I'll be home soon.*

A few seconds later, another message from Dallas popped up: *I'm kicking your ass on sight.*

Smirking, I stuffed my phone in my pocket. "I'd better get going."

Lennox stood. "I'll walk you to your car."

On the short walk, we didn't say much. Just small talk

about potholes and cold weather. I needed the distraction from the loud thoughts that wanted to pervade. Pointing to my car, I said, "That's me." I reached out to open my door, but he moved faster, opening it for me.

I hugged him. He smelled like leather, spices and almonds. I wanted to sink into him, take more of the comfort he'd offered me earlier. I wanted to… *What the hell am I doing?*

"Thanks," I whispered, pulling back.

He eyed me, his warm gaze falling to my lips. "You're welcome."

"No, really. Not just for opening the door. But for everything."

Lennox motioned for me to get in the car. "You're welcome," he repeated. "Thank you for never being predictable."

I slid into the car. "Is that a compliment?"

He raised a brow. "It definitely is."

I bit down on my bottom lip. "Are you going to tell me how you know me now?"

Lennox peered up at the sky. "Hm…" He pinned me with a heated gaze. "I think I like teasing you more."

Oh, shit. His voice…low, but soft. Every time he spoke, it tickled something deep inside me. "Really?"

"Next time."

The promise in his tone made me want to lean into him. "So, there will be a next time?"

Instead of the sexy smirk he liked to hit me with, this time he blessed me with a full smile. Dimples and all. "See you later, Blake Young."

I waved at him like a fuckin' dork. Not sexy at all. "Bye, Professor."

My place was full of people when I got there—siblings in every room, my father on the sofa, all eyes on me. Closing the door, I stood there for a second and waited.

On cue, Dallas stormed into the room and stopped right in front of me.

I apologized. "I love you?"

Dallas rolled her eyes. "I hate you, lil' punk." She pulled me into an embrace. "Don't do that again."

I wrapped my arms around her. "I won't." Eventually, I pulled back and addressed the rest of my family. "I'm sorry for my attitude lately."

A moment passed, then Duke said, "That's it. Your apology sucked."

Everyone laughed, and I ran up to Duke and hugged him, burying my face in his shirt. He smelled like *my* laundry detergent. "I'm sorry," I murmured. "You can stay here if you want."

He nuzzled my hair. "Get outta here, B. You know I'm leaving tomorrow."

I grinned up at him. "That's why you can stay." Duke waved a dismissive hand my way and walked away, letting my Dad come to me. "Hi, Daddy."

Dad rubbed my cheek. "Baby girl…" He squeezed my shoulders. "You have to do better. Jace told us what happened. We were worried sick."

"I know. I needed time to get myself together."

He nodded. "Trust me, I understand. I don't like the thought of any of you suffering or hurting."

Although my father generally displayed calmness in any situation, he'd been a fierce protector of all of us. And he'd taught us to protect each other. He'd never hesitated to put someone in their place if they'd overstepped or insulted us or tried to hurt us. I'd seen him go to bat for Tristan with the school board, beat someone's ass for disrespecting my mother, then turn around and give a lecture about understanding and unconditional love within a marriage. I knew the thought of someone hurting Bliss was hurting him. But I *also* knew he wouldn't appear anything less than in control of his emotions.

"How is she?" I asked.

"Your mother is in there with her now. She got her calmed down."

My mother had a special gift. She could sooth every ache, every bad day with her voice and her touch. That's why I'd left earlier, intent on getting Mom. While I could've just as easily called her to the house, I hadn't exactly been thinking clearly. My only thought had been that I needed to see Mom first. I needed the sound of her voice and the warmth of her touch to center me, so I could be strong for Bliss.

"Good," I whispered.

"Go see her," my father told me. "She's been asking for you."

Nodding, I walked the hallway to Bliss' bedroom. I knocked on the door and poked my head in. Bliss was lying in the bed, eyes closed, hand on her belly.

The bathroom door opened, and my mother rushed into the room. Her eyes lit up when she saw me. "Blake?" She opened her arms and I stepped into them. "Baby, where have you been?"

Words escaped me in that moment. I wanted to tell her everything, but I was just exhausted from the day.

"Sissy?" Bliss sat up. "You're back."

"Hey." I tore myself from my mother's embrace and walked over to the bed. Climbing onto it, I hugged my twin. "I'm back." I heard her soft cries in my ear and pulled back. "Are you okay?"

She nodded. "Now I am. Tyler's in jail. I'm pressing charges."

I let out a huge sigh of relief. "Good. It's time to let him go."

"I will if you do."

My eyes flashed to hers. "What?"

"You have to let go of your anger, Blake."

"I'm mad because of what he did to you," I argued. "He hurt you."

"He did. But you can't change that. You can't fight every battle for me."

My mother cleared her throat behind me. "I'm going to step out for a bit."

I glanced back at her. "Thanks, Mom."

When we were alone, Bliss said, "You're my best friend. You love me and you want to protect me. Sissy, you have. You kicked Damon Hugeley in the ass when he stole my lunch. You beat up Lindsey Hunt when she burned my cheer uniform because her boyfriend asked me to Homecoming. You told me to leave Tyler's ass a long time ago. I'm the one who didn't listen. Since you can't be mad at me, you took it out on him. And you put yourself in jeopardy to do it."

"I'm not mad at you," I said.

She smiled sadly. "You kind of are."

"I'm not."

"Blake, you are."

Closing my eyes, I leaned my forehead against hers. "Bliss, stop. I told you—"

"No. I messed up my plan, I stayed in a bad relationship, and I knew better. Because our parents showed us every day what a healthy relationship is, our father respects our mother above all else, our siblings tell it like it is even if it hurts, and my sister is The Muthafuckin' Breakup Expert."

A tear fell from my eyes. I dashed it away quickly. The lump in my throat seemed to grow with each passing minute.

"I knew better," she continued. "I didn't *do* better."

"But him hitting you is not your fault."

"It's not yours, either."

Bliss knew me better than anyone. I should've known I couldn't hide my guilt from her. "I wasn't here. I was so into myself and my feelings."

"You shouldn't have to be here. You get to be selfish sometimes. Not every time, but sometimes. We're all grown, we make decisions, we live with the consequences."

My parents had taught us to follow our hearts. They warned us that every decision we made wouldn't be right, and it was okay. They encouraged us to learn from our mistakes and be better.

"I hate him for hurting you," I whispered.

She wiped a tear from my face. "I know."

"I love you so much, Bliss. I'm always going to be here for you." I smoothed a hand over her belly and told my niece, "And you too."

"We know that too."

I rested my head on her belly. "Don't tell anyone I cried."

Bliss laughed. "I won't. Your secret is safe with me. But can I tell you something?"

I felt the baby kick under my palm. "Yes."

"It's time for you to get some."

I barked out a laugh. "You're silly."

"Like, yesterday."

"Really, Bliss? We're having this discussion right now?"

Chuckling, she patted my back. "It's time. Punishment's over."

I told her about Lennox, about our talk tonight, about the way he'd been there for me as if we'd known each other for years. "I don't know... I like him."

"Did he tell you how he knows you yet?"

I shook my head. "Not yet. He will, though. I think I like the game."

"That's something I haven't heard in a while."

"How about ever?" I retorted.

Her soft laughter sounded like music to my ears. "Right?" she said. "I don't think you've ever told me you *liked* someone before."

"I hugged him," I confessed.

Bliss' eyes widened. "What?"

Of course, I hugged my family and close friends, but I wouldn't consider myself a *hugger*. "I know. Surprised the hell out of me. I don't even know him, but he's so sweet— and male." I sighed. "And the way he handled me... I just feel different around him." I looked at her, biting down on my lip. "Weird, right?"

She nodded. "Very. There's nothing wrong with a *good* guy. And this could be a *good* thing. I need to know more."

I pointed at her. "So you can try to match us, Sissy? I'm not one of your clients."

Bliss shot me a mischievous smirk. "I promise, no matchmaking. If something happens, it'll be on you and Lennox. Not me."

"Is it wrong to want to see what he's working with before I do anything else?"

"Girl!" She smacked my shoulder.

Shrugging, I said, "I'm just sayin'! No sense in continuing if he can't put it down." Yet, even as I said that, I instinctively knew that wouldn't be the case with Lennox. Then again, I'd misjudged Dr. Donnell.

"Stop," she ordered. "You went without sex for a long time. Just enjoy the process. Get to know him. When the time is right, you'll get busy."

A knock drew our attention toward the door. Dallas entered the room. "Enough. I need to be in this room with my sisters." She climbed onto the bed, on the other side of Bliss, and pulled out her phone. Seconds later, Paityn appeared on the small screen. "I'm in here, Sissy."

Paityn grinned. "About time. I needed to see you all together." My big sister had just left town yesterday to head back to Cali. "I knew I should've stayed until Monday."

"It's okay, Tyn," Bliss said. "I'm fine."

"Blake, don't pull that shit again," Paityn warned. "I will fly my butt home and whoop your ass."

I laughed. "Such language." My big sister was never really the type to swear much. Mostly when she was irritated. She must be pissed. "I'm telling Mom."

Paityn rolled her eyes. "I'm so serious."

"I'm not as angry at you now," Dallas chimed in, "so I can say I'm glad you kicked his ass."

"If I was there, I'd give you a high five," Paityn agreed.

"Stop, you guys," Bliss said. "I have something to tell y'all."

All conversation ceased as we turned our undivided attention to her. "What is it?" I asked.

Bliss winced, then let out a low groan. "I think my water broke."

Chapter 6

PLEASE DON'T GO

Lennox

*A*t some point, life had become more about work and less about everything else. Countless hours in front of the classroom, even more time grading papers, and long conversations with students about anything from grades and sources to college events and career planning. I loved my job, I loved the students, but I found myself wanting more than this. More than lectures and syllabi and nights alone.

Past relationships aside, I liked the idea of sharing my life with someone. I wanted to have *one* person to come home to at night. I'd grown tired of the dating scene, the blind dates that didn't go anywhere, the pussy pics in my inbox, the meaningless hookups that left me unsatisfied. Since I'd broken up with Ayana, my mother's friends seemed to come out of the woodwork with nieces and daughters I needed to meet. My sisters always had a *friend* who liked me. Even Vaughn had introduced me to a producer who'd seen my TED Talk online and wanted to get to know me.

And today, I'd agreed to meet a colleague of my father's for lunch. The first ten minutes had consisted of her staring at me. We hadn't ordered our food yet, because every time the waiter came by, she wasn't ready. Right now, her head was still buried in the menu.

Pulling out my phone, I opened the chess app to the tense game I'd been playing against my father for the past few days. I studied the board, then made my move.

Seconds later, my father texted me: *Aren't you on a date?*

I glanced up at Rebekah, who was still murmuring various menu items to herself, counting calories, and reading off all the ingredients. We'd communicated via text mostly, and *she'd* chosen the restaurant because she'd claimed it had an "amazing selection of Vegan dishes." I found out later she'd only *heard* that from a friend of a friend. Bekah, as she wanted to be called, had never been here herself.

I responded: *I think Bekah is on a date with the menu, not me.*

It took a minute, but the text came through right as Bekah set her menu down: *Damn, I owe your mother $50.*

Chuckling, I shook my head. I probably should've been irritated my parents were taking bets on my love life. But I didn't bother to respond, because my date was watching me expectantly. When I met her gaze, I asked, "Are you ready to order?"

She smiled. "Yes."

I motioned for the waiter and we both placed our orders. When the server walked away, I asked Bekah, "Do you like working at the firm?"

"Yes," she answered.

Bekah worked for Cole & White Law Firm as a budget

analyst. According to my father, she'd been top of her graduating class at Stanford, played tennis for fun, and enjoyed home improvement. I wasn't sure which of those traits indicated a love match between us, though. While Stanford was impressive, I'd never played tennis in my life and I preferred to hire contractors for any home projects. In fact, I'd only agreed to the date because Dad had gone on and on about how nice she was—and because I was genuinely curious.

"My father tells me you enjoy home improvement," I said. "What projects have you done lately?"

"Oh, I haven't done anything. I like watching *Love It and List It* on HGTV."

What the hell? I sipped my water, reconsidering my choice to not day drink. "So, you like tennis?"

She nodded. "I'm not very good at it myself, but love watching Serena Williams."

Forget my mother—Dad owed *me* fifty dollars. "Serena's fly," I grumbled.

The next ten minutes were spent in an awkward silence. I went back to my game, and she stared out the window. Finally, the food arrived, and I ate as quickly as I could so I could politely end this date and maybe salvage my Saturday afternoon.

Halfway through lunch, Bekah perked up. "I saw your TED Talk," she admitted.

I eyed her. "Cool. Did you like it?"

She smiled. "I did. And…"

I waited for her to elaborate, but she just went right back to her meal. Ten more minutes passed without a word of conversation. Once again, I wondered what my dad had seen in Bekah. I wanted to ask her why she'd agreed to go out, but I knew I'd come off more like an asshole than sincere.

Any other day, I'd consider myself a nice guy. I didn't mistreat people, I always opened doors for women, I donated to causes. Giving back to my community was important to me. I gave back through mentoring and volunteering at the local food pantry monthly. But this...*is some bullshit.*

Sighing, Bekah said, "I'm sorry."

I peered at her. "For what?"

"For wasting your time. I'm not ready for a relationship right now."

"I get it," I told her.

"It's just...I broke up with my boyfriend a few months ago." Her chin trembled. "I thought it was time to get back out there. But I miss him so much." A tear fell. "I want him back."

I nodded. "Again, I understand."

"Your father talks about you a lot. I asked him how you were doing one day, and he mentioned you'd recently gotten out of a relationship, so I suggested we meet."

Her revelation made sense. My father hadn't done this on his own. Which was a good thing, because it meant it'd never happen again. "No need to explain, Bekah."

"This was fun, though," she said.

A simple "yeah" or even a "sure" would've probably made her feel better about this date. Yet, I wouldn't say either of those words, because they'd be a lie. Instead, I told her, "I've never been here before. It was interesting." The chicken burger I'd ordered was still sitting on my plate, along with the housemade coleslaw, both half eaten. The only thing I'd finished was the fruit cup.

"If you're into vegan, try Seva. It's delicious."

I dropped my napkin onto the table. "Good to know. Thanks." Another moment passed with no further exchange of words. Glancing at my watch, I said, "I need to get going."

Bekah grinned. "Oh, okay."

The server set the bill on the table. I glanced at it and stood, leaving the cash to cover our lunch.

Bekah finally slid out of her seat and hugged me, catching me off guard. As with every part of this date, the hug was stiff and awkward. "Thanks, Lennox."

"You're welcome."

She pulled back. "I'll let your father know you were a complete gentleman."

"He knows," I murmured, gesturing for her to head toward the door first. As we walked through the restaurant, I thought about what I was going to eat for a real lunch. I could go to my parents and ask for that fifty bucks and one of my mother's famous omelets. Decision made, I texted my mother and told her I'd be there in the next half hour. Outside the restaurant, I asked Bekah, "Where are you parked?"

She pointed at the Volkswagen right in front of the restaurant. "Right there. I was lucky today."

Too bad I wasn't. "Alright."

Bekah hugged me again. This time, she held on a bit longer. Uncomfortable, I patted her shoulders and tried to back away gently. Out of the corners of my eyes, though, I spotted a familiar face. *Blake.*

The smirk on her lips let me know she knew exactly what I was thinking. I mouthed, *Help me,* and she cracked up. She approached us. "Hey, Professor Cole."

"Blake Young," I said.

Bekah seemed to register I was talking to someone else, because she let go of her hold and craned her neck toward Blake. Only, she didn't speak to the woman; she simply gave her a once-over, rolling her eyes and turning back to me.

Blake's eyes widened and she shrugged, but the smile never left her lips.

"Bye, Lennox," Bekah said. "Maybe we can talk soon."

"And you can let me know how things are going with your guy."

Sighing, Bekah nodded. "Right." Without another word, she hopped in her car and drove off.

Blake inched closer to me, her arms folded over her breasts. "She's different."

Chuckling, I agreed. "You don't know the half of it."

"You looked extremely uncomfortable."

"You're very perceptive."

It'd been a few weeks since the incident at the bar, and I'd thought about Blake many times—more than I probably should've been. I didn't know her. I had no idea if she had a man or if she even wanted one. But I knew how she made *me* feel. My attraction to her wasn't surprising. Blake was a beautiful woman, with her brown skin, dark eyes, full lips. And that body… *Lovely*. Today, she wore sweats and a hoodie and she was still stunning. But it wasn't her looks that drew me to her. For some reason, I loved how her mind worked, how she expressed herself. For some reason, I wanted to protect her, to comfort her, to hold her.

"It's part of the job," she continued. "And it was all in your body language. Was she an ex-girlfriend?"

I barked out a laugh. "Hell no."

Blake grinned. "I was going to say…she's got some issues."

Curious, I asked, "You can tell from that small interaction?"

She waved a dismissive hand my way. "Man, no. I'm

not a psychic. But she did look like she wanted to kick my ass. So that told me all I needed to know."

And she made me laugh. "Sorry about that."

"It's not your fault. She's the one who would've gotten her feelings hurt if she'd tried."

"I've seen you in action. I have no doubt." I couldn't stop staring at her, memorizing every part of her—from her messy bun and the soft tendrils of hair that had fallen in her face to the tiny hoops in her ear. She wore no makeup and acted like she didn't give a fuck how she looked. *I like it.* "Are you eating lunch here?"

Blake glanced at the restaurant. "Not really. I hate bird food. I'm actually here to pick up a dozen Chocolate Cherry Scones. My family is having a late brunch this afternoon. I'm in charge of dessert."

"Ah, okay. So, you don't cook?"

She frowned. "I cook, just not today. And Bliss really loves these scones."

"How is your sister?"

Blake smiled again, and it felt like the sun had shone down on me. So bright, so warm. "She's great. I'm an auntie."

"Good. You look happy."

"I am. My niece is so gorgeous."

Like her auntie. "Got a pic?" I didn't know why I asked to see one. I just didn't want her to go.

"You know I do." She pulled her phone out. Seconds later, she handed it to me. "Isn't she cute?"

The baby *was* gorgeous, plump cheeks, head full of hair. She reminded me of my nieces at that age. "She's beautiful."

"I'm up to my eyeballs in formula and diapers and spit-up," she explained, "but I'm so happy she's here."

"Congratulations."

Blake tucked a stray strand of hair behind her ear. "I was actually going to call you."

"I wish you had."

She paused, mouth open. Clearing her throat, she asked, "What did you want me to call you for?"

"Anything," I admitted.

Blake let out a low laugh. "You're good."

"Good enough to let me take you out?"

Arching a brow, she tossed back, "To do what?"

"Anything," I repeated.

She bit down on her bottom lip. "How do you know I'm single?"

"Technically, I don't. But I hope you are."

"I am. On purpose. So my answer depends on two things."

I held her gaze. "You can set the rules of engagement…this time."

She pointed at me. "I'm not looking for a boyfriend, so don't go planning our wedding after one date."

"Do men actually do that?"

Nodding, she said, "Definitely."

Since there was no chance of me falling in love after one damn date, I agreed to that term. "Got it. Next?"

"You have to tell me where you met me."

I laughed. "I knew that was coming."

Blake tapped her foot against the ground. "Well?"

"Linc's wedding."

She gasped. "That's…" Shaking her head, she groaned. "Dallas was right. Dammit."

Frowning, I asked, "Who is Dallas?"

"My sister," she grumbled. "I owe her fifty dollars now. Were you sitting at my table?"

"Yeah. Obviously, not where you wanted to be."

"Everybody was at the other table," she said, matter-of-factly. "And I was stuck with my cousin's friend. Which is never fun."

"Why?"

"Because he wanted to hook up, and I had to tell him he wasn't my type."

I struggled to recall the person she was talking about. Other than Blake, Ayana, and two of my middle school teachers, I didn't remember anyone else at the table.

She snapped her fingers. "Now I remember. You had a girlfriend and that automatically made you off limits, which also made you forgettable. Plus, if I recall, she didn't like me."

Ayana's shitty attitude had started many arguments throughout our relationship. "She's not a factor."

"Good. Okay, then."

"Dinner tomorrow?"

She pulled out her phone again. A moment later, she peered at me with sad eyes. "I actually have plans tomorrow. What about tonight?"

"Tonight?"

"Yeah, I'm free." She frowned. "Wait—shit. I promised my mother I'd go shopping with her. But I can meet you somewhere later for a drink?"

While I wanted more time with her, *any* amount of time was too good to pass up. "Sounds like a plan. You can pick the place."

She tapped her chin. "Since I have a feeling you didn't pick *this* restaurant, I'm going to let you choose." Blake reached into her purse and pulled out her business card. "Call me?"

"I will."

"I'd better go get these scones. Oh, I forgot to tell you why I was going to call you."

I was so enraptured with her that I hadn't even remembered she'd wanted to call me. "What's up?"

"That night at the bar was crazy—and weird. I wanted to thank you again for putting my mind at ease, for giving me a safe space to get myself together."

"Like I told you then, no thanks needed."

"And since your date sucked..." She hugged me.

This hug was completely different—from Behkah's *and* from Blake's hug the night of the fight. It stirred up something inside me that I hadn't felt in so long. She wasn't embracing me because she needed my comfort. It wasn't awkward or stiff; it felt right. I wasn't looking for a way out, I wanted to hold on. The hint of raspberries and vanilla in her hair made me want to bury my face in her —everywhere.

She eased back and beamed up at me. "I have absolutely no idea why I did that."

I pulled her back to me and leaned down, so close I could feel her sweet breath on my lips. "I don't know why I did this," I murmured against her mouth before I kissed her.

We were outside and she had somewhere to be. But *damn*. Her soft moans...the way her fingers gripped the collar of my coat, the way her tongue stroked mine, the way she responded to me made me want to start our date now.

"I see you, Professor," she whispered when I reluctantly pulled away. A smirk formed on her lips. "You might be trouble."

Cupping her face in my palms, I said, "Good trouble or bad trouble?"

"Both," she breathed.

"Why?"

Her gaze fell to my lips. "I'll tell you later." She stepped into me, kissing me quickly, before she backed away. "Bye." Waving, she turned on her heels and disappeared into the restaurant.

That kiss hadn't been planned, but something told me that was how she liked it. Blake was a breath of fresh air—honest, fun, intelligent, beautiful, and sexy. And I couldn't wait to discover all of her hidden secrets.

Chapter 7

IN MY BED

Blake

"*H*ow many times are you going to change your clothes?"

I checked out my fifth outfit, twisted in the mirror so I could see my ass. "Mind ya business."

Bliss rocked Naija in her arms. My niece was officially the best baby ever. She'd barely cried, and slept more often than she was awake. "From what you've told me, Professor Cole doesn't seem superficial."

Pulling off my gray sweater, I slid on the black turtleneck I'd already tried on. "Obviously not. I looked a hot mess when I ran into him earlier, and he still asked me out." I kicked off the ripped blue jeans and tugged on black leather leggings.

Bliss gave me a thumbs up in the mirror. "Black on black is always a winner."

Sighing, I did one last twirl. "I think I'm good. I just want my butt to be thangin'."

She burst into a fit of laughter. "It is."

I pulled out my boots and walked out to the front room with her. After the heated conversation today, I wasn't sure what to expect from Lennox tonight. He'd already surpassed the expectations I didn't even know I had. And that kiss…it had been perfectly *not* enough.

"Are you staying the night?" Bliss set Naija in the travel bassinet. My twin and my niece had taken over the house. There was baby stuff everywhere—swings, blankets, pacifiers, bottles. The refrigerator was packed with healthy food and tiny bottles full of breast milk.

The question caught me off guard, because I hadn't really thought about it. Well…of course, I'd imagined sex with Lennox. But I didn't think *he* was the fuck-on-the-first-date type. He seemed like the wine-and-dine, make-his-move-on-the-*third*-date type, which was fine. I'd actively avoided sex for a long-ass time and I could handle a few more weeks.

"Probably not." I shrugged. "I don't know…I'm actually looking forward to the journey. It's been a long time since I just enjoyed a man's company. Good dessert, good drinks, good conversation. Should be nice."

Bliss sat down on the sofa and tucked her feet under a pillow. "I like seeing you excited about a date. You're always so cynical about men and dates and relationships."

"With good reason," I said. "I work with women who tell me about their nasty-ass, trifling boyfriends and husbands."

"But we know good guys. We're related to several."

"Are we including Duke in that number?" I stuck out my tongue and laughed. "Just kidding. My brother is going to be the *best* husband to the woman he falls in love with. Until then, he's going to be him."

"I still don't know why you didn't let him pick you up?" Bliss asked.

Earlier Lennox had offered to come and get me, but I'd declined for several reasons. The main one? I always reserved the right to take my ass home at any time during the first date. I fully believed in red flags, and many flew within the first hour of a date. "You know I don't do that."

"Under normal circumstances, but you've already talked to him a few times. Wouldn't you have seen some flags by now?"

Bliss had a point. Lennox had been respectful and sweet, but I still wasn't willing to give an inch on my practice. I considered it my personal easy-out clause, a safety measure—for me *and* him. "No, babe. Driving myself is necessary."

"I feel differently about this," she confessed. "Lennox seems so good for you."

I should've never shared anything about our meeting on the sidewalk today. Since then, Bliss had been waxing poetic about love and soulmates. "I think you need to go back to work, Sissy," I suggested. "You own your business. Do remote work while you're feeding the baby. Match some clients with their forever love." *So you can leave me the hell alone.*

"I've actually thought about it. I have so much time when Naija is asleep."

Opening the closet, I pulled out my black coat. "There you go. Get to work." I slipped on my boots and wrapped my scarf around my neck.

"I will," she agreed. "I'm not giving up on you and Lennox, though. I smell love in the air."

Sighing, I turned to my sister. Although she'd gone

through hell with Tyler, I was happy she still loved the idea of happily ever after—whereas I'd always been partial to the happily *never* after. "Please don't get carried away. I like Lennox as a person. That's it. I can't think beyond that. Besides, every time I think a man *might* make me change my mind about matters of the heart, he falls short on the dick."

Bliss cracked up. "You're silly."

I kissed my niece and brushed my finger over her soft cheek. *So cute.* "Alright, I gotta go." I checked my reflection in the mirror. "I'll call you when I get there."

Bye, girl."

"Bye, boo!" I shouted as I walked out the door.

LENNOX HAD CHOSEN the new black-owned cigar bar and lounge in Ann Arbor. When I arrived, he was standing outside the building with that half smile, half smirk he liked to hit me with. Dressed in black jeans and a black sweater, he looked damn good. I took a moment to check him out unabashedly.

Greeting me with a warm, tight hug and a kiss to my cheek, he murmured, "Blake." His heated gaze raked over my body, slowly igniting a fire inside that threatened to consume me. The perusal almost felt like a caress, like his hands were exploring every part of me, not his eyes. "You're stunning." The low rasp in his voice slipped under the armor I'd tried to erect before I'd gotten out of my car. And my treacherous body reacted to his touch, to his nearness.

I let out a shaky breath. "Don't start," I warned.

He chuckled—and the sound shot straight to my clit. *Trouble.* Holding out his hand, he asked, "Ready?"

Slipping my hand in his, I nodded. "Yep."

Lennox escorted me into the building, giving dap to the security guard at the entrance. The ambiance was perfect—classic décor, dim lighting, jazz band in the corner, older crowd. As we headed toward the back of the lounge, Lennox greeted several people, while I tried to avoid eye contact with one man at the bar.

Lennox must've caught my slight maneuver to his other side and he frowned. "Everything okay?"

Slipping my gaze to Colton, who was chillin' at the bar with his brother, I met his eyes. "Yeah," I lied. The last thing I wanted was to run into my ex on this date.

He seemed to accept my answer, and we made our way to a roped-off section.

Another man approached us. "What's up, Len? 'Bout time, bruh."

They exchanged some sort of secret handshake before Lennox gave him a man hug. "Figured it was high time I showed my face," Lennox said. "Blake—" he wrapped his arm around my waist, "—this is Cross. He owns this joint."

"Hey, Blake." Cross smiled and shook my hand.

Damn. Cross was fine as hell—dark skin, intense eyes, full lips. Not as hot as Lennox, though. "Hi."

Cross ushered us to a private area. A table was tucked into a nook, hidden away from prying eyes. Lennox helped me remove my coat and pulled out a chair. Once I took my seat, he sat across from me.

"I took the liberty of putting something together for your lady," Cross said. "Your usual, man?"

Lennox nodded. "Yeah."

Leaning in, I whispered, "What's your usual? And are we talking drinks or cigars?"

"Both," Lennox said.

"Bulleit, neat," Cross offered. "He's come a long way from that cheap gin we used to drink in college."

The fact that he was a bourbon man made him that much more attractive to me. And since it wasn't cognac, I said, "Nice. I'll have the same."

Cross set a box of cigars on the table. "Got it. Give me a few minutes." He walked away, leaving us alone. *Finally*.

The melodious sound of a saxophone floated in the air, setting the mood. "How long have you known Cross?" Opening the box on the table, I studied the different cigars. Admittedly, I didn't know shit about picking a cigar. Some had blue wrappers, some had gold. Some were fat and some thin. Some were long, some were short. And I was lost.

"We went to high school together, then to Howard University." He observed me silently as I picked over the cigars, still unsure what I was looking for. "Have you smoked before?"

My eyes flashed to his, and I let out a nervous giggle. "Anything? Or just cigars?"

Lennox raised a brow. "Cigars, but now I'm curious. What else do you smoke?"

My cheeks burned. In the past, I wouldn't have thought twice about admitting my occasional use of marijuana. It wasn't like I smoked a joint every day. In fact, I rarely did. But for once, I found myself questioning everything—my words, my actions. No man had ever made me second-guess myself. "I have the right to remain silent."

Lennox barked out a laugh. "But you're not under arrest…?"

Maybe I am? Taking in his scent and sitting so close to him, I felt like a prisoner—*his* prisoner. And dammit, the snarky response I'd planned to toss back evaporated under the weight of his intense stare. So, I changed the subject.

"To answer your question, I've only smoked a cigar one time, with my brother. You'll have to teach me the proper method."

Lennox stared at me. "I can definitely do that."

"Which one is your favorite?"

"Oliva Serie V, Double Robusto," he told me.

"I'll take that one," I declared with a hard nod. "I want the full experience."

He picked up one of the cigars. "Let's try something mild," he suggested, handing it to me. "Roll it gently between your fingers."

Shifting in my seat, I crossed my legs and did as I was told.

"You're feeling for lumps or soft spots," he explained, placing his hand over mine and demonstrating the movement.

The air changed around us as my heart pounded in my ears. My skin burned when his fingers brushed over mine —just from that simple touch. I felt like I was coming undone, helpless to maintain control while I was with him. *This man…* Swallowing, I asked, "If I find any, is that good or bad?"

"Bad. You want a consistent texture."

"Does it have a flavor?"

He nodded. "This one does. Mint."

"Hm." I sniffed it. "I should try this."

"Don't rush," he warned. "We have time."

For the next several minutes, Lennox gave me a quick lesson on picking the right cigar. In the end, I chose the Delicioso Black Cherry. Cross returned with our drinks, Lennox's cigar, and two rectangular ashtrays made of steel. Before he walked away, he told Lennox to let him know if we needed anything else. Once we were alone again, Lennox showed me how to cut and prime my cigar.

"Ready?" he asked.

Nodding, I said, "Whenever you are."

"Don't inhale," he instructed. "Puff."

Putting the stogie in my mouth, I went over the tips he'd given me and lit the cigar. The first puff wasn't pleasant, but I eventually got the hang of it.

Another drink and half a cigar later, I relaxed in my seat. The conversation had flowed freely. We talked about sports, history, and karate. I learned he was also a black belt, which explained why I couldn't get out of his hold at the bar. Lennox liked to play golf, watch football, and read. I loved that he was a sexy, athletic nerd—a far superior man than most of the fools who tried to holla. I also knew myself, though. I couldn't decide if I was just desperate, grateful to him, or really enamored by him. Because under normal circumstances, he would've been the exact type I'd run away from with the quickness for fear of feeling bored or stuck. Yet, I found myself enjoying him, hearing him talk about his work and his life.

We'd already established that we knew a lot of the same people. Lennox had actually worked with my father on several occasions, since they both held faculty positions at the university. And he was floored when I'd told him my niece was in one of his classes. Now, we were talking about siblings.

"Damn, eight?" he asked.

Nodding, I said, "Yes, there are eight of us—Tristan, Paityn, Duke, Dexter, Dallas, me, Bliss, and Asa. My mother went through a soap opera phase, so we were all named for a character on one of her stories."

He chuckled. "Wait a minute, I actually recognize some of those names. Duke is from *General Hospital*, Dexter is from *Dynasty*, and Asa is from *One Life to Live*?"

I laughed. "You got it. Don't tell me you watch soaps?"

Waving a hand, he said, "My grandmother watched them all. When we were kids, we couldn't talk to her during *Dynasty*. That was her show." He stared at his glass. "After she died, I tried to sit through one episode and couldn't make it."

"I don't know," I said. "I learned a lot from those shows."

"Really? Like what?"

I peered up at the ceiling, biting on my bottom lip. Then, I ticked off several reasons. "Ball gowns are perfectly acceptable for a regular dinner, shoulder pads are not what's up, no one dies when you think they do, slaps can be just as effective as a punch or a kick, sex is good in a pool, and..." I scratched my temple. "Stay away from stairs when a raging bitch is after your man or your company, because your ass is tumbling down those mugs and you will be left for dead."

Lennox grinned. "You thought about this, huh?"

Shrugging, I said, "You asked."

He sipped his Bulleit. "I have another question." After I gestured for him to go ahead, he asked, "Why are you the Breakup Expert?"

"I think we need a second date before I tell you that story." The words had come out before I could stop them. Maybe it was the bourbon? Maybe it was the cigar? I could count on one hand the men who'd intrigued me enough to even *want* a second date, let alone bring it up during the first date. More than likely, it was *him*—coupled with this place and my hormones.

Lennox picked up my hand, traced each of my fingers. "Does this mean you're going to let me see you again?"

I arched a brow. "Depends on what you want to see?"

"Anything you want to show me." He leaned forward, circling my nose with his. "Everything."

"*Shit*," I grumbled. The hint of coffee, tobacco, and bourbon on his breath was intoxicating. "I…"

My mind had already fast-forwarded to the bedroom or the floor or the front seat of the car—or that wall over there. Yet, broaching the subject, making my move, had me fucked up. Because I was in unchartered territory, wanting something I didn't think I was ready to have. But oh, damn, I *really* wanted it. At the same time, I instinctively knew a second date would tilt my world on its axis. The thought of another date, more time with him, letting him get under my skin *and* in my pants…scared the shit out of me.

"I'm on punishment," I blurted out.

Frowning, Lennox leaned back. "What?"

I blinked. "Huh?"

He smirked. "You said you were on punishment."

I sunk my teeth into my bottom lip and nodded. "I did, didn't I?" I murmured.

"You did."

Sighing, I explained, "I had a string of bad experiences and I put myself on punishment."

His tongue darted out to wet his lips. "Okay?" he prodded.

"From yak—and sex."

Raising a brow, he said, "Oh."

"It's a long story," I added, sitting back in the chair, away from his lips—and his hands. "Anyway—" I took a deep breath, "—I thought you should know that." *Lame.* Instead of well-fucked, I was just fucked up—in the head. For ruining a moment that could've ended my self-imposed drought.

Lennox pulled my chair closer to him and tipped my chin up. "Blake, if you haven't realized it yet, I want to know you." He smiled. "All of you. Punishment or not."

Having drinks with Lennox, listening to him tell me he wanted to get to know more about me, felt surreal. "Two of our interactions were crazy as hell," I said. "I broke into your house, and you saved me from going to jail. If you were a client, I'd tell you to look at the signs and run."

"First of all, you weren't going to jail, Blake. And some signs are good."

I scraped my fingernail over the edge of the table. "Still…I have to be honest, I wasn't expecting you. I'm not sure what to do with this."

"How about we change the narrative? You don't have to *do* anything. Nothing you don't want to do."

I eyed him skeptically. He was almost too good to be true.

"But just so you know," he continued, "I have mostly good intentions."

"Mostly?" I croaked.

"Since you're on punishment, I won't tell you about the bad ones right now."

I laughed. "You're silly."

"I'm serious. I'd be lying if I said I wasn't attracted to you. I think it's pretty obvious I can't take my eyes off you. While I *could* sit here and tell you I don't want you in my bed—or on my lap or in my shower or against that wall over there—that would be a lie."

I eyed the wall he'd referenced, thinking back to my own thoughts earlier, the naughty scene I'd mapped out in my head.

"But it's about more than that for me." He grazed my chin with his thumb. "Say yes," he whispered.

His lips brushed against mine. Softly first. Tentative. But when he sucked my bottom lip into his mouth, biting down on it gently, I was lost. He slipped his hand into my hair and gripped my chin with his other hand, pulling me closer and deepening the kiss. It was all tongue and teeth, moans and groans. It was everything. I'd never been kissed like this. I never wanted it to stop. Gripping his collar, I succumbed to the pull, letting him have his way with me, letting his mouth dominate mine, letting his lips control the pace, the pressure. The experience was new for me, and I liked it. Hell, I *loved* it.

When he pulled away, I could still taste him. I opened my eyes slowly. "Punishment's over," I whispered.

Chuckling, he leaned his forehead against mine. "Have dinner with me?"

"Not breakfast—in your bed?"

He searched my eyes. "Eventually."

I closed my eyes. "I told you... You are trouble."

His mouth quirked up. "I'll be good trouble tonight. After this, I make no promises."

"Okay." I smiled. "Dinner."

We spent the rest of the evening enjoying our cocktails, our cigars, and each other. And I found myself looking forward to more—*more* time, *more* kisses, *more* than kisses, *more* him.

Chapter 8

ARE YOU LONELY FOR ME?

Lennox

*W*hen I left work early on Friday, I had definite plans for my day—basketball at the gym with Vaughn and Jace, haircut, dinner and *after* dinner with Blake. What I hadn't expected was the frantic call from my mother asking for help at the food pantry. It was the second week in a row where the church had fallen short on manpower. Instead of a relaxing afternoon, I was hauling boxes of vegetables, meat, fruit, and other items for the community.

"Can you start on the boxes over there, babe?" My mother pointed to the delivery from Dearborn Ham Company. "I'm so excited we can give the first forty people in line a ham. They'll love it." She waved at someone behind me, a huge smile on her face. "Hello, welcome!"

Turning around, I was surprised to see Blake standing near the door. Whether she was dressed to impress or simply wearing yoga pants and a hoodie, she captured all of my attention. "Hey."

Blake grinned. "I figured you could use some help." She gestured to the man standing next to her. "I brought my brother, Dexter, for reinforcements."

"Lennox," I said, giving Dexter dap.

My mother clapped with glee. "Thank you so much!" She eyed me. "Is this your *special* friend, honey?"

I laughed at my mother's not-slick attempt to find out if I was dating Blake. "Ma, this is Blake. Blake, this is my mother, Paulette."

"Hi, Mrs. Cole. Yes, I'm his special friend." She winked at me before she hugged my mother. "I heard you needed a little help and I thought we'd come offer our assistance."

Over the past week, we'd communicated often. While I'd rather have a conversation in person or over the phone, Blake preferred to text. Throughout the day, she often sent random texts about anything and everything.

"Oh, yes. We could definitely use your help," my mother said. "Have either of you ever worked at a pantry?"

Blake shook her head. "No. But I'm a fast learner."

"I have," Dexter said. "In college."

My mother gave them a quick tour of the room, letting them know about the history of the program. Along the way, she pointed out the various stations and introduced them to the workers onsite.

While my mother explained something about non-perishable foods, I pulled Blake aside.

Her mouth fell open. "Hey, I'm trying to listen to the tour."

I raised a brow. "I'm sure you can figure out how to sort the rice from the pasta."

She laughed. "But what about the beans? How will I know who gets lima beans or red beans?"

Tucking a strand of hair behind her ear, I whispered, "Thanks for this, Blake."

Shrugging, she said, "Well, Dexter and I were chillin' at the office. Not doing anything. When I got your text, I figured what the hell?" She gasped, slapping a hand over her mouth. "Oh Lord, I'm in a church."

Laughing, I told her, "Hell is in the Bible."

She leaned her head against my chest. "I need to be delivert."

Unable to stop myself, I barked out a laugh, drawing the attention of a few people near us—and my mother, who was watching me with a skeptical, yet hopeful look in her eyes.

"See!" Blake whisper-yelled. "Your mom probably thinks I'm a heathen."

"Be quiet," I murmured. "She didn't even hear you."

The tour continued to the room where the church kept non-food items, such as comforters, mattress protectors, light bulbs, and other items donated by local stores. The members of the community always left the church with plenty of food and other much-needed household items.

Blake wiggled her eyebrows. "Are you ready for our date?"

Earlier in the week, after much debate, I'd agreed to let Blake pick the destination for tonight. She'd been adamant about doing something I've never done before, something I wouldn't expect to do on a date. "The question is…are *you* ready?" I tossed back.

"Of course," she said with a shrug. "I know what I'm doing."

Every time we talked, I learned a bit more about Blake.

She still held a lot close to the vest, though. But I couldn't wait to reveal all of her layers. "I believe you."

"Actually, my date idea goes perfectly with today. You'll be so happy for the treat."

Frowning, I opened my mouth to ask for another clue, but my mother zoomed in between us and steered Blake away from me before I could say a word.

Dexter approached me, hands in his pockets. "Pray real hard, bruh."

I blinked. "What for?"

"She's not good with parents." He cracked up and smacked my shoulder. "Just playin'. She'll charm your mother, and then break your heart."

I waited for him to tell me he was kidding again. When he didn't say anything else, I said, "I'll take that as a warning."

Shrugging, Dexter added, "You do that." Then he followed one of the deacons outside to start work.

As we finished unloading and sorting the many boxes, I thought about Dexter's warning. While it should've given me pause, it hadn't deterred me from wanting to know her. And when we were done with all the prep for tomorrow and Blake asked if I was ready for our date, I said, "Yes."

LATER, I was lying next to Blake—practically naked.

Blake groaned. "I don't want to move right now," she murmured. "Maybe this wasn't my best idea."

Struggling to keep my eyes opened, I said, "Actually, this was perfect."

Blake had surprised me at every turn, from the moment we'd left the church. Our first stop had been to her dojo for a light workout. Apparently, she was a little perturbed I'd been able to hold on to her at the bar, so she'd wanted to spar with me. After we'd both ended up flat on our backs, out of breath, she'd brought me to a day spa.

Lifting my head out of the face cradle, I peered over at her and let my gaze wander over her smooth brown skin, the outline of her breast against the table, the swell of her ass underneath the sheet. It could've been the soft music or the aroma therapeutic oils or just her, but I felt relaxed, sated in a way I hadn't in years. And I wanted her—all of her. All night.

The only problem? She'd put herself on punishment from yak and sex. Chuckling to myself, I thought about her panicked look when she'd told me about her promise to herself. Since then, we'd only talked about it once, and I still wasn't satisfied. Because I wanted to know more.

Her massage therapist stepped back and held up a sheet, allowing Blake to flip over on her back. I continued my perusal as the masseuse massaged her toned thighs.

"Lennox?" Her low, sultry voice pulled me from my thoughts. My gaze traveled back up her body to her face. Her eyes were closed and her lips were...*so ready to be kissed*. She smiled, almost as if she knew what I'd been thinking. "I see you."

"With your eyes closed?" I asked, turning over.

"Yes. It's my special gift."

The massage therapist applied pressure to my arms. "Really?" I said. "Can you read minds too?"

She opened those big, brown eyes, piercing me with her stare. "Absolutely."

It wasn't my style to back down, so I challenged her. "What am I thinking?"

"You're sleepy," she said.

"Of course I am."

"And you're hungry," she said matter-of-factly.

As if on cue, my stomach growled. We both laughed. "I could eat," I admitted.

"Not just for food, though."

The staff at the spa had arranged our tables close to each other, so close I could run my fingers over her body. But I wouldn't. *I'm a gentleman, dammit.* If this wasn't our second date, though... "I could eat," I repeated.

Her mouth quirked up into a smirk. "Good. Then, you'll love my plans for dinner." She blew me a kiss.

As the masseuse continued to lull me into a near-state of unconsciousness, I confessed, "I have to admit this is definitely something I haven't done before."

Her eyes lit up. "I knew it."

"You did good."

Her hooded gaze met mine again. "I'll do better later."

For much of our conversations, there had always been a hint of innuendo that could've been explained away easily. But tonight was different. Every interaction, every word spoken, seemed loaded, almost like a promise of more to come. "I'm looking forward to it. You owe me something, though."

She frowned. "What?"

"Second-date conversation."

Grinning, she sucked in a deep breath. "Really?"

"Yes."

Both massage therapists finished up and left the room so that we could get dressed. Neither of us moved, though. We stayed there, eyes on each other.

Blake sat up. "It's not a funny story." She exhaled slowly. "When I was younger, my aunt's then-boyfriend broke into her house and proceeded to beat her ass right in front of me and Bliss," she explained. "I was so angry. I tried my best to protect her. I even held the door closed while she cowered in the bathtub. Me and my little nine-year-old self. The man busted through the door, of course, and continued his assault. And I couldn't do anything to stop him."

I sensed she wanted to tell the story uninterrupted so I stayed silent, even though the thought of her afraid but fiercely protective made me want to hunt the man down now.

"I was a child," she continued, "but I knew it wasn't right. Even then, I knew that wasn't what a relationship was supposed to be. I wanted her to leave him alone." She swallowed visibly, like the memory was just beneath the surface. "Only she didn't. The next week, she was right back with him. And she stayed with him—after countless police reports, numerous side chicks. She lost everything. She was one of my first clients."

"How old were you when she left him?"

"Maybe about twelve. I sat her down." She let out a humorless chuckle. "And told her I couldn't see her like this anymore."

"She listened?" I asked.

"After a few trial runs, she finally walked away from him for the last time."

When I'd asked the question, I thought she'd tell me a story about an ex-boyfriend or one of her sister's boyfriends. Yet, as with everything I'd learned about her, nothing was like I'd expected. "Is that when you decided to become the Breakup Expert?"

Giggling, Blake said, "Actually, that nickname came about when I dumped a boy during morning recess for a girl in my class. My aunt's situation made me want to study psychology. I settled on relationship therapy, not because of my parents, but because of her. In my opinion, the biggest relationship a person has is with themselves. I believe that's why a lot of women stay when they know they should leave."

My own relationship with Ayana flashed through my mind. There were many reasons why I'd stayed with her so long, and none of them made any sense now. "I get it."

"You're the first man I've ever shared that story with," Blake admitted.

Raising my eyebrows, I asked, "Really?"

"Yeah. I don't usually show my ass—unless I'm in a sex-uation." She stuck her tongue out, then cracked up. She slid off the table and bent down to pick up the extra sheet that had fallen to the floor. "Then, you can see it, spank it, fondle it."

My gaze flew straight to that ass too. Because I defi-nitely wanted to do all of the above—and more. "I guess that means I'm your *special* friend."

Blake grinned. "Oh, God! Your mom is so sweet."

I barked out a laugh. "I get that all the time, and I always tell people they didn't live with her." Paulette Cole was not one to be played with, and she'd made that very clear from the moment I could understand words and actions. "She liked you, though."

With narrowed eyes, she asked, "How do you know?"

"She texted me."

"Ha!" She pointed at me. "You're in trouble now."

"Good trouble." My eyes dropped to her lips. The air changed around us and I wished we were at my house—or hers. "Thanks for telling me your story."

"That's not even half of it."

Still curious, I wondered if Blake's own relationship history had played a role in her choice of career. "Can I ask you another question?"

She leaned against the massage table. "Uh-oh. Maybe we've had enough Tell Time?"

"You don't have to answer if you don't want to."

"It's okay. I already know what you're going to ask, so I'll just answer." She stared at a spot behind me for a moment before meeting my gaze again. "I've never been faithful in a relationship. For a while, I thought there must be something wrong with me, something innate that keeps me from attaching to someone. I've tried, but it never works out. Inevitably, I get bored or feel unsatisfied with the commitment. So I kind of stay away from labels."

Her confession didn't shock me as much as it might have a day ago. Still, I wanted to know why. "That's…honest."

"*Too* honest for some people."

Finally, I got up and approached her. Staring down at her, I traced her bottom lip with my thumb. "I'm a grown-ass man. As long as we're honest with each other, I'm good."

"I'm glad to hear that." Blake sucked my thumb into her mouth, just one stroke before she let it go. "Are you ready for the next part of our date?"

My eyes were glued to her lips. Nodding, I said, "Whenever you are?"

Blake winked at me. "More pampering. A foot treatment."

I stepped back, hands in the air. "I object. Nobody touches my feet."

She pouted. "You'll love it."

"Nah," I said, shaking my head. "Not happening."

Several minutes later, I was seated in a chair next to Blake with my feet immersed in a bubbling bowl of hot water. And my date was cracking her ass up.

"You love it, don't you?" she said, a gleam in her eyes.

Admittedly, it felt nice. But I wasn't about to give in like that. "Don't get carried away," I grumbled. "What happens in the spa, stays in the spa, though."

Blake held up three fingers. "I promise."

Once again, I thought back to Dexter's words and the clear warning in his tone. I'd lived my life methodically, rarely stepping outside of the boundaries I'd set for myself. Relationships were no exception. When I'd chosen to get involved with a woman, it was never an easy decision but always an analytical process. Falling hard and fast for someone I barely knew was not something I ever worried about, because I'd never really invested more of myself than I felt was safe. Yet, as I sat with Blake, talking about dinner and movies and music, I couldn't help but wonder if that warning might've been a little too late.

Blake

DATES WERE CORNY AS HELL. Flowers, dinners, walks in the park, shows, lingering glances were bullshit timewasters, unnecessary detours on the way to an orgasm. But today? *This* date and *this* guy...I wanted a picture or a video to commemorate the moment because I was smitten. Unequivocally and undeniably attracted, enamored, and drawn to Professor Lennox Cole. And...*I want him.*

The entire date had been perfect, from the moment I'd entered the church, through the karate workout, through the massage and pedicure, through dinner at the seafood restaurant, through the drinks at the bar. And even now, standing at my fuckin' door. *I. Want. Him.*

But could I say that? Could I lay all my cards on the table like I'd always done when I wanted something or someone? My hard rules had been thrown out the window the minute I'd agreed to pick *and* pay for the date, the minute I'd agreed to spend time wracking my brain over the smallest of details. The challenge had been clear, and I'd accepted with no reservations. Because I'd wanted to surprise him, I'd wanted to give him a night he'd never had before. Technically, *I* was new to him, so sex would be unchartered territory, but still…

"Did you want to come in?"

"I had a nice time."

The sentences were said simultaneously, but his sentence was less naughty and more nice.

"Sure."

"Me too."

Shit. More awkward same-time comments.

I gripped his wrist. "Come in." Unlocking my door, I stepped inside and turned on the light. Scanning the room, I was pleasantly surprised Bliss had removed all signs of her and Naija from the living room before she'd left to spend the night at my parents' house. Instead of baby powder, I smelled jasmine and vanilla. I set my purse on a table. "Can I get you anything to drink? Cognac, vodka, tequila, beer…?"

"Cognac is fine."

Lennox wandered around the living room, checking out the art on my walls. He'd shared his love of art with me on our first date and his attention was immediately drawn to the Aria Jackson painting on my wall.

After I poured two drinks, I walked over to him. "Stunning, isn't it?" I handed him a glass.

With his attention still on the art, he murmured, "Beautiful."

Staring at him, I thought about how beautiful *he* was— his face, his smile, his body, his spirit. *Shit.* What the hell was wrong with me? Waxing poetic over this guy, and I hadn't even seen his dick? I felt the back of my neck. *No fever.* I gulped the entire glass of Hennessy and almost tumbled back on the couch. Embarrassed, I pretended to fix the pillows on the sofa.

Lennox gave me a sidelong glance. "You okay?"

Clearing my throat, I nodded. "I'm good."

Finally, he turned his intense gaze on me. And I melted. At this point, it was embarrassing how much I wanted him, how much I wanted to drench myself in him. The sound of the refrigerator, the faint scent of my favorite candle, the artwork in front of me seemed to fade away. All I could see or hear or smell was him.

I glanced at my empty glass and figured a little more cognac was in order. Turning, I started toward the kitchen, but his hand on my wrist stopped me. And I waited— waited for him to do something, to say anything, to touch everywhere.

I dropped my head and stared at the edge of the area rug, at the imperfection I'd caught when I'd brought it home months ago. I wasn't a novice. I knew how to get fucked. But, for some reason, I always fumbled with Lennox.

"You're trembling," he whispered, taking my glass from me and setting it down on an end table.

"I can't stop," I breathed.

He stepped into me. I felt his breath against my ear and the hard ridge of his erection. "You have a decision to make tonight, Blake."

I bit down on my bottom lip as my heart pounded in my chest and my nerve endings sparked to life. *Damn.* The way he said my name… Closing my eyes, I took a few cleansing breaths.

"This connection," he continued, "is deep, unexpected. But very real."

Swallowing, I nodded. "True."

He grabbed my hips, holding me against him. Nipping the lobe of my ear, he murmured, "We could have another drink, talk about anything you want for an hour. Then, I can go home."

"Or?" I asked.

"Or I could…"

"Eat?" I felt the tremble of his laughter against my back, prompting me to chuckle too. I turned in his arms. Shrugging, I said, "What? You said that earlier, and I thought it was appropriate now."

Tipping my head up, he searched my eyes. "If that's what you want."

I kissed him, sucking his bottom lip into my mouth until he groaned. His hand closed around my hair as he took control of the kiss—licking and biting and stroking. I couldn't get enough, not when he lifted me into his arms, not when he carried me over to the counter, and not when he perched me on the edge. And certainly not when he dropped to his knees, peeled off my pants, ripped off my panties, and buried his face in my—

"*Oh, shit.*" Yes, I said that out loud. No, I didn't care. Because his tongue, his mouth, his lips devoured me like I was his first and last meal. I held his head there, not willing to let him go, and let him have his fill. Sensations overloaded and overwhelmed me, and my legs started to shake. A delicious orgasm snuck up on me, crashing into me so hard I couldn't breathe, I couldn't think, I couldn't feel anything but him.

Unable to hold myself up, I fell back against the counter, weak and drained. His lips were still on me, though—on my legs, on my inner thighs, on my clit. I came again on a tortured sigh, trembling as pleasure rolled through me one more time. He pulled me upright and kissed me. His mouth was hot against mine, his tongue demanding. But I liked it. Hell, I *loved* it.

Picking me up again, he tossed me over his shoulder in a fireman's carry and walked through my house, down the hallway, stopping at each room before he stepped into my bedroom.

My back hit the mattress seconds later. He pulled my shirt off and tossed it behind him. Stepping back, he stared at me, his heated gaze raking over every inch of my body.

I sat up, beckoned him with my forefinger. "You are so much trouble, Professor Cole."

He hit me with that smirk again. "Good or bad?"

"Both. And that's alright with me."

He gripped my legs and pulled me to edge of the bed. I unbuttoned his jeans and pushed his pants and underwear down. *Damn.* This was the only part of him I hadn't seen, thanks to that massage. And he didn't disappoint. Not at all. It'd been so long, I didn't know what I wanted to do first.

After a short internal debate, I leaned forward, took him into my mouth, and licked him from base to tip.

He groaned. "Shit."

Keeping my eyes on him, I cupped his balls in my palm and sucked him in again. I repeated the motion again, then again, closing my eyes as the feel of him inside my mouth took over. I wanted to drive him as crazy as he was making me. Yet, before I could take him in once more, he stopped me.

Gripping my chin in his palm, he shook his head slightly. "I let you control the date. I'm in charge now."

As disappointed as I was, I couldn't do anything but fall back against the mattress and let him have his way with me. He started at my feet and kissed his way up my body to my breasts. He gave each of my breasts equal attention

113

until I cried out his name and begged him for more. Every kiss, every brush of his hands against my sensitive skin, branded me. I was slowly unraveling, slowly letting him steal pieces of myself that had once been off limits.

"Lennox," I breathed. Begging was not my thing, but a soft plea was on the tip of my tongue because I wanted him inside me, I wanted his body against mine.

"Open your eyes," he commanded softly.

I did as I was told and met his waiting gaze. He gripped my hips, sinking inside me. Bending down, he brushed his lips over mine. It was so tender, so soft, I whimpered. Me? Whimper?

With his eyes on mine, he moved, out and in, over and over. Our slow, deliberate pace quickly turned fast and passionate—mouths fused together, arms wrapped around each other. When I climaxed, the force of my orgasm felt like it would split me in half. *So good.* And Lennox was next, growling out my name as he came.

Moments passed with no movement, no words. Finally, Lennox kissed my neck and rolled over on his back, pulling me into his arms. After-sex cuddling was a no-no for me, but I couldn't stop myself from snuggling into him. I couldn't stop myself from wanting more of him. And I couldn't stop myself from laughing.

He pulled back and glanced at me, a frown on his face. "What's funny?"

"Nothing." I kissed his chin. "I was joking the other night, but now I can definitely say my punishment's over, because I had yak *and* sex tonight."

He chuckled, tracing my jawline with his finger. "You're silly."

"You can go ahead and say it now."

"Say what?"

"That my date kicked ass. You loved every part of it."

Smiling, he admitted, "It was cool."

I raised a challenging brow. "Even the foot treatment?"

"Yes, even the foot treatment."

"I think I deserve an award."

He tapped my nose. "Don't get carried away."

"I'll take breakfast tomorrow, though," I added.

"Does that mean you're not kicking me out in a few minutes?"

I gasped. "Oh shit, I forgot. You're already past your twenty-minute limit." He tickled me, and I cracked up. "Okay, okay. You can stay."

"Good answer."

Resting my head on his chest, I wrapped my arms around his waist. Time stretched on, and I made no move to get up or make an excuse for him to leave. I was content to lie there, to let him hold me. Because for the first time in a long time, I wanted to be held.

Chapter 9

DO WHAT YOU DO

Lennox

*M*ost of us were out here figuring shit out. As much as I tried to rise above things, be the bigger person in any situation, there were times when I wanted to fuck some shit up. *And I did.* Because no matter what I'd done to protect myself and my reputation, the mere allegation of inappropriateness on my part could potentially destroy my life.

Therefore, when another professor had slipped into my Hip Hop and Sociology Class to "observe," I knew something wasn't right. Everything had started out as planned with a brief discussion about the lyrical analysis paper before I segued into a discussion on the early history of hip hop and its influence on the Black community during the crack epidemic. Unfortunately, his presence had distracted some of the students—especially when he'd raised his hand to ask two questions that had nothing to do with the topic and everything to do with me and my teaching methods.

Things went downhill from there, culminating in a full-blown argument—about Dory. The woman was wanted by the police, yet she'd still managed to turn my world upside down with her bullshit. And even though my Department Chair, the authorities, and most of the faculty believed me, that one damn professor had made it his mission to help Dory get justice. Which meant he was coming for my job.

"Maybe you shouldn't have cussed his ass out?" Emerie shrugged when I glared at her. "Just sayin'."

Vaughn sipped his beer. "Nah, you definitely should've cussed him out. You did good to not beat his ass."

Emerie's mouth fell open. "Vaughn." She smacked him. "Don't encourage that type of behavior."

I gave Vaughn a pound. "Believe me, I thought about it."

"But then you'd be in jail," Emerie said. "And Dad would've never let you hear the end of it."

They hadn't said anything I didn't already know. From the time I could reason, my father had told me to "never let a muthafucka pull you off your square." And he'd promised that I'd have to deal with him if I did get caught slippin'. I'd taken that lesson with me in high school, in college, and beyond. I knew better than to let a colleague get under my skin.

Vaughn rubbed the back of his neck. "Man, I'm not scared or anything. But your Pops… I still remember when he mopped the floor with me after I challenged him to a boxing match."

Glancing at my watch, I laughed. "I told you to shutcho ass up that day, but you didn't listen." Vaughn had had a tumultuous family life growing up, and as a result had a huge chip on his shoulder that my father had been happy to knock off. "Always talking shit."

Shrugging, Vaughn said, "I learned that day."

"What did Dad say when you told him what happened?" Emerie asked, leaning forward.

"You know what he said," I told her, recalling the short conversation I'd had with my father after I'd left the office today. Pops had immediately turned into Jeffrey Cole, Esquire. By the time I'd gotten off the phone, I had a legal plan of action mapped out and an attorney from his firm retained. "Loren is representing me."

"That's good." Emerie squeezed my hand. "Everything is going to be okay, Len. Dory will be a bad memory in a matter of weeks."

Checking the time again, I murmured, "I hope so."

Vaughn eyed me skeptically. "What's up, bruh? You late to something?"

"Nah, man."

"You do keep checking your watch," Emerie pointed out. "Are you waiting for someone?"

Blake had shocked me when she'd agreed to join us for dinner. Up until now, we'd been in our own little world, choosing to spend time with each other and avoiding group situations. She'd stated she didn't want the pressure from her family to define our relationship. For my part, I wanted her to myself. I'd taken advantage of every hour, every second I'd spent with her, exploring her mind and her body. And it still wasn't enough. I always wanted more of her.

Clearing my throat, I muttered, "I invited someone to dinner."

"Your girlfriend?" Emerie asked.

"A *friend*," I corrected.

Immediately, Emerie hit me with a barrage of questions. Where was she from? Was she pretty? Did I like her? Were we serious? "I mean, you have to tell me something?" she said. "You invited her to dinner without telling us. I want to know all about her."

"Maybe he'll answer a question if you stop talking, baby?" Vaughn suggested.

I let out a deep breath, relieved my best friend caught my need for a reprieve. "Her name is Blake," I shared. "We just started hanging out. Nothing serious." *Yet.* "And that's all I'm telling you."

"Bet," Vaughn said. "Let's eat."

Emerie rolled her eyes and elbowed my best friend in the gut. "Don't play me." She folded her arms over her chest and told me, "I'm not satisfied with that answer. I need to know more."

Needing a change of subject, I leaned back. "Enough about me. What's up with y'all? I thought we weren't seeing you until the summer?"

Emerie shared a glance with Vaughn and took a deep breath. "We do have news."

"Is everything okay?" I looked at Vaughn. "Do I have to kick your ass?"

Grinning, Vaughn shook his head. "Nah, bruh. Nothing like that."

Emerie clapped. "We set a date!"

"I want you to be the best man," Vaughn added.

Vaughn had proposed to my sister last summer, but they'd both been vague about the details, much to my mother's dismay. And since Emerie lived on the other side of the country, Dana and I had to hear all about it—in every phone call or visit to my parents' house.

"'Bout time," I said. "You know I got you."

"Thanks, bruh." Vaughn shot Emerie another sidelong glance.

"What am I missing here?" I asked.

"We're getting married in three months," Emerie blurted out.

With wide eyes, I said, "What? Are you pregnant?"

My sister waved a dismissive hand my way. "No, but we're moving—" she swallowed visibly, "—to the UK."

"I booked a world tour," Vaugh explained, "and Emerie landed a solid job in London. So we figured we'd make the move."

Vaughn was a popular DJ who'd toured with several high-profile R&B and Hip Hop artists. And Emerie was an up-and-coming DJ who'd built quite the reputation in the short time she'd been doing it full-time. It wasn't uncommon for them to travel abroad for gigs. But moving overseas?

While they didn't live near me now, I wasn't sure how I felt about my little sister moving out of the country. And if *I* was apprehensive, I could only imagine how my mother had taken the news. She still had her heart set on a church wedding and more grandkids running around her back-yard. "How did Mom take it?"

"She cried," Emerie admitted. "She's not happy."

Usually, when Emerie or Dana needed reinforcements to convince my mother to abandon her plans, they called on me. "And you need me to talk to her?"

Pressing her hands together as if she were praying, she said, "Please? I don't want her to be angry for too long. I'd love to enjoy my family at the wedding."

Nodding, I agreed to smooth things over with Mom. "Wow," I said. "London, huh? Are you sure about this?"

Emerie beamed. "Len, it's a great opportunity, and I want this. It's not forever, but it's for now."

It had taken a lot for my sister to leave her stable job as a respiratory therapist to follow her dream of becoming a

DJ. I was proud of her for taking the risk, and as I'd always done, I would give her my blessing. "Okay," I told her. "You know I'll support you any way I can."

Tears filled her eyes as she stood and walked over to me. "Thank you!" She held out her hand. "Love you."

I stood and hugged her, kissing her brow. "Love you too."

She pulled back, dabbing at her cheeks with her thumbs. "I'm not really crying. But I should probably fix my face." Emerie blew a kiss at Vaughn and excused herself.

Once she was out of earshot, I took my seat again and said, "I'll still kick your ass in London," I muttered.

Vaughn barked out a laugh. "Whatever, man."

"I'm serious, bruh. Take care of my sister."

"No doubt."

Despite my many warnings to my best friend, I knew he wouldn't hurt my sister. I'd seen the love between them and I'd watched their relationship grow in so many ways. I had no doubt they'd take care of each other, and I looked forward to following both of their careers.

"So what's up, man?" Vaughn asked. "'Who is this mystery woman?"

Laughing, I said, "You've been around Emerie too long, bruh. This is not what we do."

Vaughn nodded. "You got a point. Did you fill out your brackets? Who you got for the Final Four?"

Our March Madness tradition had never waned, even though Vaughn lived elsewhere. Each year, we'd put up our money and bet on our picks. "I don't know yet," I confessed. "Still debating between Michigan and George-town." Last year's pot had been enough to pay off my car. This year, I hoped to continue my winning streak and get my roof replaced.

"I like Michigan State. The Big Ten is strong this year."

Emerie reappeared right before I clowned Vaughn for his choice of teams. She plopped down. "Woo, that bathroom is off the chain."

I glanced over toward the door just as Blake entered the restaurant. Standing, I told them I'd be back. Blake had recently returned from a weeklong trip to Hawaii for a family wedding, and she was a sight for sore, tired eyes. As I approached her, she was peering at her phone, a slight frown on her face. I took a moment to look her over. Her hair was pulled back and her skin was glowing, probably from all the sun she'd been treated to on her trip. She wore dark jeans, a sweater, and boots. Casual, but still fine as hell.

When she spotted me, she smiled. "Hey!"

"Blake?" Some dude crossed over to her and pulled her into a hug. "It's been a long time."

She met my gaze, then addressed ol' boy. "What's up, Kevin?" she said, her voice flat.

"When are you going to let me take you out?" he asked. "It's been a while."

"On purpose." She eased out of his hold. "I told you I'm not interested." Without another word to him, she walked over to me. "I'm sorry," she breathed. "That was…weird."

We'd never made any promises to each other, so I had no idea if Blake was seeing other people. Yet, the thought of her with someone else pissed me the fuck off. "Very," I grumbled.

"I'm sorry," she repeated. "I'm so late. I tried to get here on time but I had to stop at the office."

"It's cool. How was your flight?"

She shrugged. "Long. I slept a lot, though." Tilting her

head, she searched my eyes. "Are you okay? You sounded weird on the phone earlier."

"I'm good," I lied. Having another conversation about the drama of the afternoon and Dory was definitely not something I wanted to do.

"Sure?"

"Yes," I assured her.

"I forgot to warn you. I'm good with parents, but sisters? I don't know about that."

Laughing, I brushed a strand a hair behind her ear. "You'll be fine."

"That's what they all say," she muttered. "I—"

"Hey, sexy," another guy whispered, cutting in.

Blake's shoulders fell. "Keon, hey."

"My mother asked about you the other day. Maybe you could come to dinner over at the house one Sunday?"

She flashed a polite smile. "I don't think so. But tell your mom I said hello." Turning away from him, she looked at me. "Ready?" On the way to the table, someone else called her name and she ignored him. She leaned closer and whispered, "I promise this never happens."

Chuckling, I said, "I believe you."

"Seriously, Lennox." She stopped, peering up at me. "I'm not really—"

"Blake, it's okay." My gaze fell to her mouth. The urge to kiss her, to claim her in front of every last person in that restaurant, welled up inside me. Letting out a slow breath, I said, "You don't have to explain yourself to me."

"But…" She sucked in a deep breath. "You're right. It's fine."

We finally made it to our table and I introduced Blake to Emerie and Vaughn.

"Hey!" Blake hugged both of them. "It's so good to meet you."

"You too!" Emerie grinned widely. "I love your hair."

"Thanks." Blake slid into the booth. "I'm so sorry I'm late."

Emerie waved a hand. "Girl, please. I know how it is."

As if they'd known each other for years, my sister and my...*friend* fell into a conversation about curl patterns and keratin treatments, only pausing to place their food orders.

Picking at her hair, Emerie said, "I miss the salon. I haven't been to one since I recognized my ex-boyfriend's dick on someone's smartphone."

I nearly choked on my beer. "Really?"

"That was you?" Blake asked. "Kerry is my stylist too. She'd squeezed me in that day. I heard the whole thing."

Emerie cracked up. "I was so embarrassed, Kerry started doing my hair at my house. I guess those are the perks of having a best friend who's one of the best hairstylists in the city. I still haven't found a stylist I like in LA."

Blake sipped her water. "Well, you shouldn't be embarrassed. Men are full of shit. I'm just glad he's your *ex*-boyfriend."

I glanced at Vaughn, who was watching the two of them segue into a conversation about trifling men and messed-up relationships.

"What do you do?" Emerie asked after another round of drinks arrived.

"I'm a relationship therapist."

"She's The Breakup Expert," I added.

Emerie's mouth fell open. "Wait, you're Blake Young? I read your article."

Blake nodded. "Yeah."

"You're out here changing lives, Blake. Shit, have you told Kerry to leave that fool she's been dealing with alone?"

Rolling her eyes, Blake said, "I been telling her. I'm not

too worried, though, because it's not that serious for her. She keeps telling me she's holding out for her friend's… brother." Pointing at me, Blake asked, "Is that you?"

"Yikes," Emerie whispered, sinking down in her seat a little.

It was no secret my sister's best friend had harbored feelings for me, but nothing had ever happened between us.

"Yeah, it is," Vaughn offered.

Blake eyed me, a smile on her lips. "Interesting."

Leaning in, I whispered, "What have you heard?"

She pulled away, batting her eyelashes. "You'll never know. Stylist-client confidentiality."

Dinner arrived a few minutes later, and we settled into safer talk about sports and travel. Over near the bar, I noticed a man staring at the table and wondered if I knew him. More time passed and every time I glanced up, that same guy was watching us. I wasn't a paranoid person, but after my interaction earlier, I considered that maybe he was following me trying to get some sort of evidence of wrongdoing.

Just when I was ready to confront him, he stood and walked over to us. But instead of addressing me, he called Blake's name.

She stiffened next to me. "Colton? What are you doing here?"

"I saw you sitting here looking stunning and figured I'd come say hi."

"And you really interrupted my dinner?"

"Maybe when you're finished, we can talk," Colton said. "Get a drink?"

Closing her eyes, Blake let out a heavy sigh. "This cannot be real," she mumbled. "No, we cannot have a drink. But you can have one by yourself."

"Blake, if you would—"

"Bye, Colton."

"Awkward" wasn't quite the word I'd use to describe what had just happened. Unlike earlier, though, I wasn't pissed. I was more concerned about her, because she looked upset.

Blake dropped her napkin on the table. "I have to... I need to take care of something. I'll be back." Grabbing her purse, she slid out of the other side of the booth and walked toward the door.

"What the hell just happened?" Vaughn asked.

"Duh?" Emerie said. "She's embarrassed."

I stared after Blake as she bulldozed through the crowd near the door and walked outside. "For what?" I asked my sister.

"Please, you can't be this dense. She agreed to meet your sister, which means something. And since she walked in the door, random men have been approaching her like she's not with you on a date. Then that jackass came over while we were in the middle of dinner? She's probably mortified. I know I'd be."

"I don't care about them."

"So! *She* cares about *you*. And she probably doesn't want you to think bad of her. You should go see about her, Len." Emerie suggested. "Oh, and invite her to our wedding. I like her."

Turning over Emerie's words in my head, I stood and grabbed my coat. I found Blake pacing outside of the building, her head down and her hands flailing. She was muttering something under her breath.

I stopped right in front of her. "Hey."

She froze. Without looking at me, she grumbled, "Hey."

Taking her hand, I pulled her into my arms. It took a minute, but she finally hugged me back. "Blake, I—"

"Don't," she warned, smoothing a hand over her hair. "What the fuck was that?" She shrugged. "It sure as hell wasn't normal."

Amused and unable to help myself, I smiled. "You're really upset about this, huh?"

"Yes!" she shouted. "I'm pissed."

"Listen, we've both had past relationships. The only thing I care about is what's happening between us right now."

She let out a shaky breath. "I'm really not a hoe."

Chuckling, I said, "I know you're not a hoe, Blake." I tugged her back to me and kissed her. "But I like that you care what I think."

Her eyes softened. "I do," she whispered.

"Then, let's move forward." The statement could've been referencing tonight or forever. I didn't bother to specify. "Finish dinner, have dessert…"

She smirked. "At your place? You'll be safe. I won't be taking any vases or anything."

"I'm not worried." Although we'd spent the night together after the spa date, we hadn't had anymore overnights since then. That wasn't to say we didn't find ways to be together—in her office during lunch, in my car, at the Oasis Hot Tub Gardens, in the private sauna at the gym… We'd definitely made it a mission to get it in as often as possible. "You can give me my shirt back, though."

Blake cracked up. "Oh, you're not getting that back. A shirt for a shirt. You ruined mine, so I get to keep yours."

That happened the second time we'd made love, in my SUV before dinner one evening. Needless to say, we never made it into the restaurant that night. "Touché." Grabbing her hand, I led her back to toward the door. "Speaking of my shirt, I want to see you in the one I have on now. And nothing else."

"Beat you there." Blake sprinted toward her car.

Pulling out my phone, I sent Emerie and Vaughn a quick text letting them know we were heading out and then took off after Blake. Everything my sister said made sense, and Blake's actions and words had confirmed it. Meaning this thing between us wasn't as casual as we'd tried to make it, as *I'd* tried to pretend it was. Which was fine with me, because I cared about her too. And I needed her to know that.

Chapter 10

IT KILLS ME

Blake

*W*aking up with Lennox's fingers in my pussy and his mouth on my clit was *the. Best. Thing. Ever.* Letting out a hoarse cry, I came for the second time that morning and collapsed against the mattress.

"So good," he whispered, kissing his way up my body, paying special attention to my nipples before he sucked my bottom lip into his mouth.

Soon, he was inside me, simultaneously pulling me apart and putting me back together again. We made slow love this time, pushing and pulling, nipping and sucking. I reveled in the feel of his body against mine, the sound of his dirty words in my ear, the smell of his skin, and the way he filled me up like no other man had before—physically and emotionally. Climaxing together, we clung to each other as if we'd never have another moment like this again and knowing we definitely would.

Once I was able to catch my breath, I burrowed into his side, which was fast becoming one of my favorite places to be. I fit perfectly there, snug in his warmth. I didn't want to move; I didn't want to burst the bubble we'd created with each other. But I had so much to do today.

Pressing my lips against his chest, I murmured, "Is it too much to ask for another day like yesterday?"

After skipping out on the rest of the dinner with Emerie and Vaughn, we'd returned to his house and spent the rest of the evening and the next day wrapped around each other, making love leisurely between meals and snacks.

Lennox tipped my chin up and planted a tender kiss to my lips. "You could always stay?"

It was tempting, lounging around with him. But it was Sunday, and I had work to do. Groaning, I said, "I wish, but I can't." I kissed him again and sat up, picking up my phone. As expected, I had several missed calls and terse text messages from my family. I spent a few minutes sending *"I'm fine, see you later"* texts to everyone who'd contacted me, except for Paityn.

My big sister had sent a text telling me to expect a surprise package soon, to which I replied: *I hope it's not nipple clamps. That shit hurt.*

Paityn had been steadily building her sex toy business and had always used us as her guinea pigs, sending us everything from whips to sex swings. And I was here for all the kink—except for the nipple clamps. Hard pass.

To my surprise, and in spite of the three-hour time zone difference, Paityn responded: *No. You'll love this one. Trust me. Call me when you get it. Love you.*

Lennox's hand smoothed up my back, sending chills up my spine and making me want to fall back into his arms. Closing my eyes, I set my phone down and sighed. I'd told myself many times that this wasn't serious, that I was just having fun. Yet, the more time I spent with him, I found myself helpless to resist him and wanting to abandon my plans for another kiss, another touch. I glanced back at him, studied his profile. He didn't look at me, didn't speak. His gaze was on the ceiling, but I suspected his thoughts were somewhere else, definitely not in the room.

I placed my hand on his chest. "Are you okay?"

"One of my colleagues wants an investigation opened into this Dory allegation," he said.

Turning around, I inched closer to him. "What?"

He told me about an altercation he'd had on Friday after one of his lectures. Apparently, Dory had managed to convince one faculty member to believe her, which had prompted an investigation from the Dean of the College of Literature, Science, & Arts. "I have a meeting with the Department Chair tomorrow to discuss a plan of action, and an administrative hearing with the Dean next month." He met my gaze then. "This could take me out of the classroom, ruin my tenure track. All because this woman knows how to lie."

I struggled to find the right words to say to him. If this had happened to me, I'd be devastated, angry, vindictive… all of the above. "I'm sorry," I croaked.

"Why did you believe her?" I opened my mouth to say something, but he rushed on, "Because I heard what you said before about how she was referred to you, but I need more than that. Was what she'd said *really* that believable?"

My cheeks burned and I averted my gaze. In hindsight, Dory had never been *that* believable. Her story had just triggered something from my past, brought to mind my own traumatic experience in college, and I'd run with it. I knew better.

"Blake? Look at me," he commanded softly.

Hugging my knees to my chest, I hunched my shoulders. "When I was in college, my Abnormal Psych professor approached me after class and invited me to dinner. When I turned him down, he became belligerent, threatening...violent."

"Did he...?"

Shaking my head, I said, "He didn't sexually assault me. But he grabbed me and, of course, I defended myself with a knee to the groin and right upper cut. He retaliated in the classroom by flunking me, spreading lies about me to students and other faculty. He was well-respected, had been with the U since the Seventies. And he thought he could get away with it because my parents were out of the country. Fortunately, my father has a lot of pull with the university and made his own threats. Eventually, the man lost his job, but the damage was already done to my reputation." And unfortunately for Lennox, Dory had said the magic words—*he's ruining my name*.

"It was a trigger for you," he said.

I nodded. "At that point, it ceased being about Dory. It wasn't even about you."

"I'm sorry that happened to you."

My stomach fell. Even when he should've been worried about himself, he was concerned about me. It made me want him even more. "Nothing Dory said was believable. From the very beginning, her story didn't make sense to me. I'm ashamed I reacted the way I did. And I intend to write a bomb letter to the Dean outlining my experience with Dory."

"You'd do that for me?"

"Of course. I'll talk to my father too."

He wrapped a hand around my calf. "Thanks, for offering to help and for telling me your truth."

132

"Since I'm talking, I want you to know I've never been so happy to be wrong about someone."

He laughed. "I'm happy you were wrong too." Pulling me to him, he kissed me. "Thanks, baby."

Baby? It wasn't the first time a man had used that endearment for me, but it was the first time I'd liked it. "The truth will come out, and you'll be vindicated. *That* I believe."

"I hate that there's even a question. It's not who I am."

I stared into his eyes, struck by the sincerity shining back at me. "I know." My eyes fell to his lips. Leaning forward, I kissed him. "You're everything she's not—sane, kind, honest. So much more."

He smirked. "Be careful, Blake. I think you're starting to fall hard for me. Pretty soon, you're going to want me to be your boyfriend."

Starting? The word hung in the air. Because I wasn't starting anything. I'd already fallen. And it scared the shit out of me.

"WHAT DO YOU THINK?" Duke asked. "Think I could make it happen?"

Duke and I strolled through a local mall. He'd just taken me on a tour of the site where he wanted to do a couples cooking class a few times a month.

I sipped the spinach-and-kale smoothie he'd purchased for me. Nodding, I said, "What types of things will you do in the class?"

Duke explained he'd have a different theme for each class, giving couples an option to learn a variety of dishes. "I figured I'd start with Tuscan cuisine or Italian, something simple and light."

Eyeing him skeptically, I said, "Italian is not light. I always fall asleep after I eat pasta."

He grabbed my cup, took a sip from it, and gave it back to me. "If this goes well, I might set up something down in Atlanta too."

"Or you could always move back to Michigan?"

Although Duke visited a lot, he hadn't lived here in over a decade. And despite our penchant for arguing, I missed him. He'd never treated me like his helpless *little* sister the way Tristan had, and he'd always been brutally honest with me about everything, unlike Dexter, who often tried to sugarcoat shit. Duke had dragged me with him to parties and hipped me to the games men played when they wanted booty. When I'd lost my virginity, Duke was the first person I'd told. After he'd yelled at me for wasting it on Keon, he'd sat me down and taught me some things about life and men and making shitty decisions. He was one of my favorite people and we were extremely close.

He snorted. "Yeah, no. I'll fly my ass here when I want to see y'all or when I need to work."

Laughing, I bumped into him. "You know you miss us. That's why you keep showing up unannounced."

We passed the furniture store and I stopped to admire a butler ottoman that would look fabulous in my living room. I started to drag Duke into the store when I spotted Lennox over by a sectional. He wasn't alone, either.

"Don't buy that ottoman, B," Duke said. "That's something Mom would buy. Man, I swear. You'd better not turn old-fashioned on me."

"Shut up," I grumbled, watching Lennox and his mother talk to a salesperson. When I'd left him this morning, he'd mentioned meeting his father to discuss the Dory situation, but I'd never expected to see him with his mother.

"What are you looking at?"

"Lennox," I admitted.

As if he'd heard me, Lennox turned, and I rushed out of view, dropping my damn smoothie in the process. With narrowed eyes on me, Duke picked up the cup and tossed it in a nearby trashcan.

For a long moment, he didn't say anything. He just stared at me—in his annoying, *see-all* Duke way. My brother was the most talented of the group, a child prodigy of sorts. He'd excelled in art, music, food, math, science… everything. He was the most like my father when it came to matters of the mind, which was why he'd once considered a career in psychiatry. But his love of cooking had propelled him to abandon medical school after his first year. Instead of becoming Dr. Duke Young, he'd enrolled in the Culinary Arts Academy in Switzerland and had never looked back.

Unable to take his silent, unwavering assessment anymore, I asked, "What, man?"

"I'm trying to figure out why the hell you're hiding from him," he said, his eyes cold. "Did he do something to you?"

I rolled my eyes. "No. Lennox hasn't done anything to me." Except treat me with respect, make me tremble with need for him, and crack me up when I didn't feel like laughing. "I just spent two whole nights with him, I don't want him to think I'm stalking him or anything."

Duke looked around. "We're at a strip mall. You're not hiding in the bushes outside of his house. Who the fuck cares if you ended up at the same place?"

"I do," I snapped, unsure why I cared so much about what Lennox thought of me. Sagging against the wall, I said, "I just don't want him to see me. Stop asking so many damn questions."

"It's not like you to hide. If this guy makes you want to hide, what the hell are you doing with him?"

I let out a heavy sigh. "It's not like that."

"Tell me what it's like." Duke's eyes softened, and a slow smile spread over his face. "Wow."

"What?"

"You like him."

I groaned. "Shut the hell up. You get on my nerves."

"Blake Young is actually infatuated with someone." He peered into the window and frowned. "Wait, are you jealous of the woman he's with or something? Because she looks old enough to be his momma."

I shoved him. "That *is* his mother, fool."

Duke laughed. "I'm just playin' with you." He folded his arms across his chest. "Seriously, what's the problem? You obviously like hanging out with him—you spent nights with him at his place. Go talk to him."

"I'll see him later."

"Stop acting like a lil' punk."

"I will if you stop acting like Ayanla, trying to fix my life." Lennox walked out of the store at that moment, holding the door open until his mother emerged. "Let's go."

"Blake!" Duke shouted, pushing me toward Lennox and his mother.

Mrs. Cole waved at me and they headed our way. I glared at my brother. "I'm going to fuck you up when we get home." Turning to them, I plastered a smile on my face. "Hi!" I hugged his mother. "Fancy meeting you here." I peered at Lennox. "Hi."

He smiled. "Hi." Leaning down, he kissed me.

And I didn't flinch, wince, or spin away from it. I simply kissed him back. *Go figure.* Duke shot me a knowing glance because he'd caught that shit too. I introduced my brother. "He's in town on business," I told them.

Lennox gave Duke dap, and Mrs. Cole shook his hand. "Good to meet you," my brother said.

"So you're one of the triplets?" Mrs. Cole asked. During my stint at the church food pantry, she'd given me the third degree about my family. And since Duke and Dexter were practically the spitting image of each other, it wasn't hard to put it together.

"Yes," Duke replied. "Have you met Dallas yet?"

"No, but I met Dexter," Mrs. Cole explained, a proud grin on her face. "He helped us at the church food pantry. Lovely young man."

"I may have to check the food pantry out on my next visit." Duke glanced at Lennox. "Blake was just telling me about you."

Raising a brow, Lennox said, "Really?" He grinned. "That's good to know."

Earlier, Duke had correctly surmised that I was falling for Lennox, and now my brother had just confirmed I'd been talking about him. I was in trouble. "Yeah, I was just..." I stammered. "We were looking at that ottoman, and, um..."

Duke cut in, "She'd already told me you two had been spending a lot of time together and then she spotted you in the window."

"We have," Lennox said, not taking his eyes off me.

"Good, good." Duke nodded, his gaze moving from me to Lennox, then back to me. "I'm piloting a cooking class for couples next month. You two should come."

Mrs. Cole clapped. "Great idea. Yes, you two should go."

"Fun," I said through clenched teeth, because I had no

intention of going to that damn class, and my brother had essentially locked me in without permission.

Lennox chuckled, as if he knew exactly what I was thinking. "Yeah. Keep me posted on the date."

Mrs. Cole glanced at Lennox. "I'll go call the restaurant to place our dinner order. Would you two like to join us for dinner?"

I blinked.

Once again, Duke slid in with the save. "We'd love to, but we have dinner plans at our parents' house. But next time I'm in town, how about I cook dinner for everyone?"

"Sounds wonderful," Mrs. Cole said. "It's a date."

"Great," Duke said.

"Well, we'd better let you order your dinner," I said lamely. "It was so good to see you again, Mrs. Cole."

"I hope to spend more time with you, Blake," the older woman said.

I nodded. "Definitely." I met Lennox's gaze. "I'll talk to you later?" This time, I kissed him, surprising the hell out of myself. Pulling away, I scratched the back of my neck. "Yeah, um... Bye."

"Bye."

I watched them walk away. When they were finally out of sight, I glared at Duke. "Don't say anything." Then, I stalked off toward my car.

Chapter 11

OUT ON A LIMB

Lennox

*T*he term "crazy" about something or someone had always seemed foreign to me, impossible really. But standing in the middle of Blake's living room watching her simultaneously work, blow on her niece's belly, help Bliss pack a diaper bag, answer texts from her family, and get dressed for her brother's cooking class... *I'm definitely crazy about her.*

That was just the tip of the iceberg, though. Blake was stubborn. She'd refused to call me anything other than her *friend*. It had started as a joke, something we'd both laughed about after my mother had given her the moniker months ago. Now, it bothered the hell out of me. Because I felt like she was mine. Everything about her—her body and her soul—was mine. I wanted to go to sleep next to her every night and wake her up with an orgasm every morning. I wanted to give her and this *non*-relationship everything I had. I wanted to take things to the next level. And I was willing to jump through hoops for her.

"Did you hear me, Lennox?" Blake bounced her niece in her arms.

"Huh?"

"You weren't even listening." She tilted her head. "Are you okay?"

"I'm good," I told her. "What's up?"

"We can go as soon as Bliss gets off her call, okay?"

I nodded. "That's fine. No rush."

Blake bit down on her lip. "Well?"

Confused, I asked, "Well, what?"

"How did it go today?"

After numerous letters from faculty, strong statements from Blake and her father, and an outpouring of support from my students, the complaint against me had been dismissed and the matter was officially closed. "Better than I expected," I said, telling her about the hearing. "The Dean even apologized for everything. Dory will never be permitted to take a class at the university again."

Beaming, Blake hugged me. "That's good! Now if only I had a chance to beat her ass. Any word from Jace on her whereabouts? Tristan had to turn his attention to another case."

"Not yet." Dory had managed to thwart authorities. But I knew she was still around, waiting and watching. It was only a matter of time before she was caught. And that day couldn't come soon enough.

Bliss emerged from the bedroom. She smiled at me. "Hey, Lennox." She greeted me the same way she always did—with a wave and a kiss on the cheek.

"Hey." I'd gotten to know Bliss pretty well over the past few months. I definitely understood why Blake was so adamant about protecting her. She was sweet, giving, a beautiful person. And she'd fallen into motherhood seamlessly.

Blake handed the baby to her sister. "I just changed her, and the diaper bag is all packed."

Smiling at the baby, Bliss said, "Thanks, Sissy. I'm late. I have to drop her off with Mom so I can make it to the cooking class on time."

"You'll be fine," Blake told her, hanging the diaper bag on Bliss' shoulder. "Duke will wait to start. It's just us."

"Jace still coming?" I asked.

Bliss shrugged. "He said he was. If he doesn't, I'm not staying."

"Bliss!" Blake shouted. "You can't leave."

"Oh, I can. And I will. I'm not that chick who hangs out with a bunch of couples."

"First the fuck of all, don't think of it as a couples thing. No one is bringing a boo." She winced, meeting my gaze. "Sorry."

"I'm not your boo?" I asked, raising a challenging brow. *I'm sick of this shit.* I considered myself a patient man. I rarely lost my temper, I didn't yell, and I'd never disrespected a woman. But this woman—*my* woman—was gone learn today. We were having this conversation, and I didn't care if Bliss was there to hear.

"Lennox, you know I talk too much." Blake shrugged. "I didn't mean it that way."

I folded my arms over my chest and pinned her with a glare. "No, I heard you loud and clear."

"Um." Bliss scratched her forehead. "I'm just going to leave now. Bye."

"Wait," Blake said. "We should just walk out together. If you feel better, we can take you to Mom and Dad's and you can ride with us in case Jace doesn't show."

"Nice try," I interjected.

Bliss sighed. "This is awkward."

"Jace will show because he's not an asshole," I assured Bliss.

"You're right," Bliss said. "We've been friends for years. He'll be there, and I'll see you both later."

Blake grabbed the diaper bag. "I'll walk you out."

I picked up the baby carrier. "*I'll* walk her out." Then, I gently took the bag from Blake. "And I'm coming back to finish this."

Bliss waved. "Bye, Sissy."

Following Bliss to the car, I strapped the baby in. Once the car seat was secure, I opened the driver's side door for her. "See you in a little bit."

"Don't be mad," Bliss said. "She does talk too damn much."

I laughed. "She'll be alright."

"Just so you know…she really does care."

"I know." I watched her pull out of the driveway and waited until she sped off before I walked back into the house.

Blake was sitting at the breakfast bar, her legs crossed and a pretty frown on her face. "Look, Lennox, you—"

"No, you listen." I walked over to her and spun the chair around. "What the hell do you think is happening between us?"

"We're getting to know each other," she said.

"That's it?"

Blake opened her mouth to speak, then closed it. I suspected it was because she knew she was on some bullshit. She stood and tried to walk away, but I pulled her back to me and caged her in so she couldn't leave.

"Tell me, Blake. What is it?"

"Are we really doing this right now? We're going to be late."

"You're always late," I countered. "Why is today different?"

"It's not."

"Then tell me," I repeated. "Why are you resisting this?"

"I'm not resisting *this*." She motioned between us. "You know I want you. I think that's pretty obvious. We talk every day, we sleep together, I spend the night, you're here now."

"But I'm not your boo."

"You're my boo, okay!" she shouted. "You're more than my boo. But, honestly, I…" She swallowed visibly. "It's overwhelming how much I want your mind and your body. I want you *too* much."

"That's a problem for you?"

"Of course it is."

It wasn't funny, but I couldn't help but laugh. "How is that a problem?"

"Because it just is."

"It's not," I argued. "I know what the problem is."

"What is it, then? Since you know everything."

"You. You're overthinking it." Unable to help myself, I kissed her. Hard. And slow.

She sagged against the counter. "You did that on purpose."

I nodded. "I did. Because I'm sick of this shit. There's no question here. I'm your guy. You're my girl."

"No."

"No?" I laughed.

Her gaze fell to my lips. "It's not that simple." She ducked under my arms and bolted to the other side of the room. "I make a living being The Breakup Expert. My credibility is based on the fact that I'm a badass single woman and okay with it. I'm trying to ride the wave of *It's*

Not Me, It's You all the way to the bank. I already have a book deal, and I'm trying for a movie deal. When my clients see me, they want that snark, that *fuck-all-men* candor. I can't ride off into the sunset with you and be happy. I have a brand to protect."

"Bullshit." I approached her. "You've created a persona that's been very lucrative for you. I get it. But why does that mean you can't be happy with someone? Make that make sense, because it just doesn't."

She rested her hand on her forehead. "We have to go."

"No, we're going to finish this."

"And if I say no, we're not?"

"Then, you can go to the cooking class by yourself."

Blake muttered a curse and plopped down on the couch. "Fine, Lennox. I don't know what you want from me."

"It's not obvious to you?"

She gave me a sidelong glance. "Maybe not."

"I've been clear in my intentions from the very beginning. I don't think anyone expects you to stay single so your fans feel better about breaking up with their boyfriends or their husbands." I sat next to her and pulled her on my lap. "I know you care about me."

She lifted her eyes, holding my gaze. "I do."

"You said you didn't know what I wanted from you. Well, I need something more than this *we're friends* bullshit. Can you give me that?"

She nodded. "I'll try."

I nipped her chin, then kissed her. "Try hard."

Smirking, she said, "I'll try really hard tonight."

"At the cooking class?"

"And after the class." She batted her lashes. "Now, can we go?" She stood up.

Smacking her ass, I said, "Let's go."

144

. . .

WE WERE VERY LATE to the cooking class. Duke was in the middle of his presentation on the different types of pasta when we finally took our seats. Most of her siblings were there. Even Paityn and her husband, via Zoom.

Luckily, Blake knew how to cook, because we were able to jump in without missing a beat. By the time we were done, we'd prepared strip steak with a white wine sauce, potato gnocchi with basil pesto, an arugula salad with homemade dressing, and mint chocolate gelato.

Now, we were all seated around a large table. Conversation was lively and indicative of the close bond Blake and her siblings had with each other. I felt at home with them and appreciated how welcoming they were.

"Stop. My steak is just fine," Dallas argued.

"If you like charred food," Dexter retorted. "And runny gelato."

Dallas tossed a piece of bread his way. "Shut up. You just worry about your *not*-done steak and your bitter lemon-parmesan dressing."

"Mine is tasty," Paityn announced.

Everyone's attention flew to the television screen. "That's because you're a mini-chef yourself," Asa murmured, stabbing at his steak with his fork. "Not all of us are talented in the kitchen, big sis."

Jace and Bliss were huddled together, cracking up about something in private when Duke asked, "What the hell are y'all kee-kee'ing about?"

Blake elbowed me. "I'm so glad he showed up," she whispered, eyeing the scene as Duke and Bliss went back and forth with each other about minding one's own business.

I sipped my drink. "I told you he would."

Jace had never bothered to hide how he felt about Bliss to me. In fact, it appeared everyone knew except for Bliss. Yet, no one had mentioned it to my knowledge.

"What are you whispering about?" Dallas dipped her fork in Blake's plate and stole a piece of her steak.

Blake smacked her hand. "Don't touch my food, heffa. And stop worrying about what we're talking about and pay attention to *your* date."

Shrugging, Dallas said, "Your steak is pretty, and Preston is not my damn date. He's filling in that friend spot while Cooper is falling in love and shit down in Rosewood Heights."

"Friends, huh?" Blake asked.

"Yeah. Like you and Lennox. Right?" Dallas arched a brow.

The entire table went silent. Suddenly, all eyes were on us. I glanced at Blake, who was conveniently gulping down her wine. She finally set her glass down and said, "Lennox and I are more than friends."

"More than friends?" Duke asked. "Care to elaborate?"

"No, nigga," Blake growled. "I said what I said."

"Really?" I asked.

Blake sighed. "He's my man, okay?" she announced. "Eat." Without warning, she kissed me. "I told you I'd try."

I laughed. "Good job."

"Are you happy?"

"Yes." I squeezed her thigh.

"Great. Now, you can take me home and show me how happy you are?"

After we said quick goodbyes, we rushed out. It took less than twenty minutes to get to her place and only two minutes to get her clothes off once we were inside.

"Take these off," I commanded, hooking a finger into the waistband of her black lace panties.

Blake pouted. "I'd rather you do it."

I shook my head. "Nah, I want you to do it. Slowly."

She turned around, glancing at me over her shoulder. "How slow?"

"Very." She flashed a wicked smirk and took her time removing her panties while I dropped my pants and pulled off my shirt. Spinning her around, I dropped to my knees and brushed her clit with my thumb. When she cried out for more, I sucked it into my mouth. It didn't take her long to come and when she did, her knees buckled. But I didn't let her fall. *I'll never let her fall.*

A smile spread over her face as she purred contently. "I love your type of trouble, Professor Cole."

And *I* loved when she called me Professor. "Turn around," I ordered softly. "Bend over."

Her hooded eyes met mine and she turned, bending over the couch. I smacked her butt again. Slipping a condom on, I stepped into her, held my dick at her entrance, and pushed my way in. I closed my eyes, loving the feel of her around me. We fit together, as if she was created just for me.

"Please," she breathed. "Lennox."

I'd intended to take my time with her, to enjoy her body a little longer. But my need for her wouldn't let me. Instead of slow and tender, our lovemaking was hot and hard, frenzied and fast. I couldn't get enough of her, of her taste, of her smell, of her voice. And when she came with my name on her lips, I let go, coming so long and so hard I nearly took us both down to the floor.

I rested my head on her back, struggled to catch my breath. After a few minutes, I scooped her up in my arms and carried her to the bedroom. I set her on the bed and climbed in behind her, pulling her close to me.

She kissed my nose, then my mouth. "I'm so sleepy."

I'm so in love. The realization hit me like a brick. But there was no other explanation for how I felt, how she made me feel. Just being with her tonight had cemented it. My parents had often told us about how patient and kind love was, how all-encompassing it was. And despite their example, I'd never really connected with the idea of unconditional love. It had always felt too big, so impossible to attain. But Blake...our relationship was bigger than my doubts. And I wanted to feel it, I wanted to give in to it and make her mine. Forever.

Blake

IT WAS OFFICIAL, waking up next to Lennox *was* my favorite thing to do. And I'd done just that almost every morning since he'd made me call him my *more than a friend*. That was almost a month ago, and we'd continued to speed past the point of no return.

Lennox was like a drug. Being with him gave me a high I'd never experienced before. I couldn't breathe, I couldn't see anything but him. I was addicted to him, lost in him. It had taken over everything, had me doing shit I'd never done like spending the night, cooking dinner, and answering calls even when I didn't feel like it.

I felt stuck, torn between running *from* him and running *to* him. But my desire for him had surpassed any notion of walking away completely. I just wanted more. Which was why I needed to take a step back, to clear my mind from the Lennox Fog that had taken over my life. It didn't take long to convince my sisters and my mother that we needed a girl's weekend, so as soon as I saw my last client, we were hopping on a flight to Cali.

Yet, even though I'd initiated the trip, I felt guilty. I hadn't told Lennox I was leaving. Not after we'd made love this morning, not after we'd eaten breakfast together, and not after he'd brought me lunch an hour ago. I knew I was wrong, and I was going to tell him. Really. Before I left. *I promise.*

"Blake?"

I glanced at the couple in front of me. Granted, I'd checked out of the last fifteen minutes of our session, but I'd already heard enough to make my assessment.

Leaning back in my chair, I crossed my legs. "Please don't take this personal, but you ain't shit. I've been listening to you for an hour, blaming your wife for your shortcomings."

Frowning, Mr. Howard shifted in his seat. "Excuse me?"

Every once in a while, I had a client who really got on my damn nerves, someone who made me want to fight them. Mr. Howard was that guy, and today I had time to tell him what an asshole he was. "Sounds like you're the one with the problem. You work all day, sleep all night. You don't take your wife anywhere other than the grocery store. You hate everything she cooks, you hate her family, and her kids. You can't fuck, don't suck…what the hell are you good for? Why are you still there? Hell, why are you even here? You're obviously not that interested in your wife, so why don't you do everyone a favor and leave?"

Fuming, Mr. Howard jumped up and pointed at me. "I

don't have to listen to this, Blake Young. And I will be telling your father."

I shrugged. "Good. Tell him I'll be over later for dinner."

Pivoting on his heel, Mr. Howard stomped out of the office and slammed the door.

Glancing at his wife, I said, "I'm sorry, Auntie. Excuse my language, but I just couldn't take it anymore."

Aunt Faye sniffed into the tenth piece of Kleenex she'd grabbed in twenty minutes. "Blake, you shouldn't have done that."

"You deserve better. Do you really want to be with this man forever?"

Against my better judgment, I'd agreed to let my aunt bring her husband to one of our sessions. I counseled women on leaving, not mending relationships. Yet, I couldn't resist the woman who'd taught me how to write my name in cursive, the woman who'd pressed my hair, the woman who'd bought me pancakes from McDonald's every other Saturday because I loved them. Obviously, she wasn't ready to leave her trifling second husband alone, and I hated to see her like this week after week—dejected, whiny, and sad. As much as I loved her, after today, she'd need to find a *marriage* counselor or a clinical psychologist.

"I know it's over," she said. "I just didn't want to admit it, and I definitely don't want to go through a second divorce."

I squeezed her shoulders. "It's okay to walk away. You've proven that, time and again."

She shot me a wobbly smile. "It doesn't feel like that, Blake. Every relationship I've had has failed."

"Because the men you're choosing are not worthy of you. I've been telling you that since I was a kid."

My aunt hugged me. "I'm so proud of you. Not just

because of how successful you are, but because of *who* you are. You saved my life all those years ago when Walter kicked my ass. You stayed on me, encouraged me to get out of that toxic relationship. And you've continued to set an example of a strong woman."

"You're strong too, Auntie. You've persevered, and you've never given up on the fairytale."

She wiped her nose. "I won't. Even after everything that's happened, I still believe in love and happy endings."

I laughed. "That's where Bliss gets it from, huh?"

Grinning, she nodded. "I guess so. But you can have it too, baby."

I swallowed. Getting to happily ever after had never been something I'd considered. I'd told myself I didn't need it, that I didn't need a man to make my life complete. In hindsight, I could recognize the lie hidden in all that false bravado. Because underneath my happily-*never*-after persona, I was just scared. Terrified to open myself up, to let someone in, to get hurt. *I'm still scared.*

"I'll call Dallas and set up a meeting." Aunt Faye pulled me into an embrace. "I love you."

"Love you too."

I walked my aunt to the door. After we said our good-byes, I called Lennox and asked him to stop by after his last class.

Fifteen minutes later, my admin poked her head into the office. "Blake?"

"Hey, Lexie," I said. "What's up?"

She stepped into the office and closed the door. "You have a client."

"I'm done for the day."

"You might want to see this woman." Walking over to my desk, she set a Post-It down. In big letters, the name

"Dory" was scrawled on it. "She's right outside, tells me her name is Hannah."

I scribbled a note for her to call Jace. "Okay, I'll see her. Send her in."

Lexie hurried to the door and ushered Dory into the office before she disappeared, hopefully to call the police. I popped a piece of candy into my mouth and stood.

"Hi," Dory said.

"Hannah, huh?" I kicked off my shoes, just in case I had to kick her ass. "What are you doing here?"

"You're with Professor Cole."

Planting my hands on my desk, I asked again, "What are you doing here?"

"I saw you with him. You were walking at the park, hand in hand. Then, I saw you leaving his house. I saw him entering your place. Why are you with him?" she shouted.

It occurred to me in this moment that no one had really told this girl the truth. She'd lived her life thinking the world was hers for the taking, that she could have anyone, that she could do anything without consequences. "I don't owe you an explanation for what I do or who I do it with. You're wanted by the police. Yet, you're here— upset about a man who's never been yours. You created an entire relationship with your professor; you nearly destroyed his career. Yet, you're here trying to check me for some perceived offense."

"You told me you'd help me."

"That was then. Now, I'm telling you to go fuck your-self. You put my business and my license in a fucked-up situation."

"I came to you for help," she said through clenched teeth. "You said you believed me. And then you take him from me?" Tears streamed down her face. "He was mine first."

As angry as I was at Dory, her mental state concerned me. She was a danger to the community, but more so to herself. I glanced at my watch and prayed Jace would get here soon. "You need help, Dory," I told her. "*Professional* help."

Dory stomped toward me, but before she made it to my desk, Jace stepped into the office with two officers. While Dory shouted obscenities and hurled threats, one of the officers handcuffed her, and the other read her the Miranda Rights.

Jace approached me once the officers escorted Dory out. "Are you okay?"

"Yeah," I said. "She didn't do anything, but she's not well."

"I'm surprised she showed up here."

I shrugged. "I'm not. She saw me with Lennox. Jealousy made her careless."

He squeezed my shoulder. "I have to get down to the station."

"Thanks, Jace."

Lennox entered the office, a frown on his face. "You okay?" He shook Jace's hand. "I just saw them walking Dory out."

Jace excused himself, leaving us alone.

"I'm fine," I said. "I know how to protect myself."

He ran his finger down my cheek and pulled me into a hug. "I know, baby." He pulled back and searched my eyes. "What did she do?"

I explained the situation to him. "The more she talked, the more it became apparent she needs more than punishment. As much as I wanted to kick her ass all up and through this building, I couldn't bring myself to do it. She's troubled, and she needs psychiatric help."

"You did the right thing," Lennox agreed.

Wrapping my arms around him, I kissed him. I poured my all into that kiss, clinging to him like a lifeline. When I pulled back, the words were on the tip of my tongue—*I need you, I love you.* But I couldn't bring myself to say them. Instead, I brushed my lips over his again.

Lennox groaned, and that sound made me want to make love to him right here. "You taste good," he murmured against my mouth.

"Jolly Ranchers." I kissed him again. "Grape."

"What did you want to talk to me about?"

This was why I didn't want to tell him I was leaving. Because I knew that once I saw him, I wouldn't want to go. Because I was dangerously and hopelessly in love with Lennox. My eyes burned as tears threatened to fall. And I was also an emotional wreck. "Um—" I swallowed past the hard lump that had formed in my throat, "—I wanted to tell you I'm going to Cali to see Paityn."

He frowned. "Okay?"

"Today." I looked at the wall clock. "In a few hours."

He stepped back. "And you're just now telling me this?"

I fiddled with a paperweight on my desk. "It was a spur-of-the-moment decision. I need mommy-sister time."

"Are you okay?"

Dammit. He was so good, so sweet…so sexy. "I'm fine."

It was an outright lie, because I wasn't okay. I messed around and fell in love. And now I had to figure out what to do about it.

Chapter 12

U GOT IT BAD

Lennox

*T*he Winter semester ended without fanfare, and the Spring semester started with several full classes, a waitlist for the Fall semester, a new book deal, booked speaker engagements, and a Mentorship program that promised to be fulfilling for years to come. My career was back on track, but my personal life... Did I want to move forward with Blake? *Of course.* Yet the mechanics of making that happen, the reality of our situation, and her obvious fear made it a harder question to answer.

I knew what I wanted. And when Blake was with me, I knew what *she* wanted. When we were together, we were in sync, on the same accord. But Blake wasn't here now; she hadn't been here for days. With little notice, she'd left town for *mommy-sister* time. Which wouldn't have been a problem for me under normal circumstances. I wasn't that guy. I didn't need to police my partner, know her whereabouts ·

every single moment of every day. I did want to be respected, though. While I'd never require her to tell me everything, I *wanted* her to share her life with me. I wanted to build a life with her.

A knock on my office door pulled me from my thoughts. My father poked his head in. "Son?"

Smiling, I stood. "Pops. What brings you by today?"

My father's office was located a short five-minute walk away from my office, but he rarely stopped by in the middle of the day. Our busy schedules had prevented spontaneous visits. I welcomed his presence, though, because I needed the distraction.

He took a seat. "Your mother told me to get in more walks during the day, so I figured I'd see if you were free for lunch. My favorite hot dog vendor is back."

I laughed. "When Ma told you to take walks, I'm sure she didn't intend for you to eat greasy smoked sausages and salty chips."

"Ah," he grumbled, waving a dismissive hand my way. "I won't tell if you don't."

My stomach growled, and I met his amused gaze. "I guess I could eat right now."

With temperatures in the low seventies and plenty of sun, it felt like spring had finally arrived. The bipolar weather in Michigan had tricked us many times through April, but the temperatures had held steady since the start of May.

My father bit into his sausage and groaned. "This is good." He stared at it lovingly. "I should've bought two."

I laughed, taking a bite of my much-smaller hot dog. "It does hit the spot every now and then."

We ate in silence as we walked back to my office building.

Once he finished, he tossed his trash into a bin and

wiped his hands with a napkin. "How are you feeling about the situation with Dory?"

Jace had contacted us yesterday to let us know she'd managed to post bail. "I knew she wouldn't be in jail long. The prosecutor told me they'd pursue the aggravated stalker charges in court, but I'm not holding my breath for a long sentence or anything. It's not like she committed murder. And, honestly, I just want her to get help."

"Well, we'll see how it plays out in court. And security?"

"I added a few cameras outside my house. But I'm not going to live my life watching the bushes or anything."

"And you shouldn't." He finished his bottle of water. "Anyway, enough about her. I want to throw your mother a surprise birthday party."

My mother was turning sixty in July and she'd never had a birthday party. Not that we hadn't tried to plan anything for her through the years. We'd actually tried several times, and she'd always nixed any plans we'd made, preferring to spend her day quietly. "She's not going to like that," I said.

"I don't care. I want to celebrate her in front of every damn body we love. She deserves it."

I grinned. "As long as we can blame you, I'll help any way I can."

He barked out a laugh. "Don't worry. I'll handle your mother. I've already talked to Dana and Emerie. They're ready to help. I think we'll do it at the Detroit Institute of Arts. She loves it there."

"Sounds like a plan."

"How's Blake?" he asked.

Over the years, my father had been my sounding board. I'd always been able to go to him about anything, without judgment. I hadn't talked to him about my relationship with Blake at all. They'd met each other. She'd been to my parents' house for Sunday dinner and had even volunteered at the pantry several times.

Still, his question surprised me. As with everything else in my life, my father usually waited until I broached a subject with him before he brought it up or gave advice. Giving him a skeptical glance, I said, "She's okay. I guess."

"I don't like the sound of that, son."

"She left," I admitted.

He frowned. "Left you?"

"Nah, left town. To visit her sister."

"Ah, okay. So you're a free man this weekend."

Despite her assurances that we were no longer on the *special-friends* track, I couldn't shake the feeling that she was still running from me, that the prospect of being together had her shaking in her boots. I didn't like it. "I'm a free man every day," I mused.

Pops stopped walking and pointed at a nearby bench. "Have a seat."

A moment later, I joined him on the bench. We sat and watched the passersby as they hurried to their destinations. Most of the students had gone home for the summer, and campus was pretty quiet. To my right, a tour guide was leading a group of high school students through the courtyard. A group of friends were skateboarding, oblivious to everything except their course.

One of my students shouted, "Hey, Professor Lennox!" She walked over to us. "I signed up for one of your classes this fall."

"That's good. Be prepared to work, Maia. It's not going to be easy."

She laughed. "I know, I know. But I'm excited."

We talked about summer reading material for a few

minutes and I recommended a lecture series she might enjoy.

When she walked off, my father chuckled. "You were always so focused on your end game, whether you were building something with your Legos, finishing a science project, competing in a karate tournament, or even playing video games."

I smiled to myself, thinking about one particular conversation we'd had about my inability to have fun. I must've been six or seven years old when my parents sat me down and told me I had to quit reading club to play baseball on the youth league. My little ass had been heated, but I'd ended up having fun. That was the summer I'd met Vaughn. That was also the summer I'd discovered girls weren't disgusting.

"I've watched you with Blake," he continued. "You were focused on her too. And I told your mother...she's the one."

I met his gaze. "You got all that from a Sunday dinner?"

"I know you. Besides, it's in your eyes. I recognize the look, because I see it every day in the mirror. You're just like me. Quiet, intelligent, determined..."

"I don't agree that you're quiet, though."

My father's low chuckle settled something in me. He had a way of centering me. "I'm quiet when I need to be. I also watched the way you two interacted with each other, the way she makes you laugh, the way you let her be who she is. I felt it, because that's what your mother and I do for each other. You love her."

Dropping my gaze, I nodded. "I do."

"So what's the problem?"

My parents had married at the age of twenty, against everyone's wishes. And they'd been supporting each other through everything since. Their example was inspiring, but it felt impossible for me right now.

I hunched a shoulder. "She's not ready. She has this idea in her head that she can't be who she is within a relationship."

"That's not true."

"I know that, but she doesn't. I thought we were moving toward the same destination, but when she left…I don't feel good about it."

He nodded. "Have you talked to her?"

"Yeah." The few brief conversations had cemented the feeling in my gut that something was off between us. There was no substance in the interactions. We'd only talked about surface things, and that was a deliberate choice—on her part. "She's scared. What am I supposed to do with that?"

"If she's scared, then you have to be her safe place. Eventually, the fear won't dictate her choice, because she'll know you're steady, that you're going to love her through her mess. No relationship is perfect, but it can be pretty damn close if both of you are committed to it."

"And if she doesn't let me love her through it, how do I justify hanging on? At some point, I'll resent her."

He squeezed my shoulder. "If you love her, then you love *her*. Have a conversation with her, son. Talk it out. Trust me, it's worth it."

I thought about my father's words. I loved Blake; I loved everything about her. And I couldn't let her go without a fight. "Thanks, Pops."

Standing, he glanced back at me. "You know I'm always hear to listen—and tell you when you're wrong. I'd better get back to the office, though. I have a client meeting in an hour."

We headed back to my building, discussing the

upcoming NBA playoffs. When we arrived, I noticed several students running out the doors. I scanned the immediate area. People had started to gather outside. "What's going on?" I asked no one in particular.

"Fire," one young lady said. "On the fifth floor."

"That's my floor," I told my father.

One of the office assistants came barreling out of the building and ran straight to me. "Professor Cole, your office is on fire. I tried to get Julia to come out, but she's still gathering some of your things."

My stomach tightened as dread took over. My gut told me this fire had everything to do with Dory. Exchanging a glance with my father, I noted the worry in his eyes. "Call Jace." Then, I took off toward the building.

Blake

"I so needed this."

I glanced at Paityn, who was floating next to me. Our short weekend trip had morphed into a week-long vacation. I'd enjoyed my time with my mother and my sisters—shopping, eating, talking…my kind of escape. "Me too," I said.

"I'm thinking we should go with tacos tonight," Bliss suggested.

Today, we'd decided to chill at Paityn's new beach house, since Bishop was out of town on business. And I couldn't wait to eat more of Paityn's food. I missed her culinary skills. "Sounds good to me," I agreed.

Staring up at the blue sky, I tried to concentrate on

the moment, the quality time with my favorite women. But my mind wandered to Lennox; it *always* wandered to him. At the mall, at the Salsa Club, during dinner, while I was sleeping… Apparently, I was incapable of *not* thinking of him. Despite what I'd told myself, I missed him so much. I hated myself for leaving the way I had, but instead of fixing it by talking to him and assuring him I was fine, I'd continued to act like an asshole. We'd talked a few times, but it was never enough. And that was my fault, because I'd let my fear make the choice for me to leave.

"I fucked up, Tyn," I whispered.

Paityn glanced over at me. "I was wondering when you were going to talk about it."

"Really?"

"Girl, please. I know you love me, but planning an impromptu trip to see me is not the Blake I know."

"I'm spontaneous," I argued.

"But you're not a planner."

Dallas walked over to the edge of the pool and sat down, swinging her feet in the water. "Are we talking about this now?"

"Yes," Paityn replied.

"Mom!" Dallas shouted.

Bliss set Naija into the travel swing we'd brought along on the trip. "It's about time."

"What's going on?" my mother asked, stepping onto the patio.

"We're talking about it," Dallas waved her over. "Come on."

Soon, my mother was seated next to Dallas and Bliss, and all eyes were on me. A moment passed. Sighing, I blurted out, "I fell in love." All of them clapped, and I cracked up. "Wow!"

Paityn gripped my hand. "That's good. See, it wasn't that bad to say it out loud."

"Actually, it was."

"Sissy, it's okay to love him. I fell in love, and it's amazing."

"Of course it is. You're you," I told Paityn. "You live for this stuff—cooking for your man, giving massages, telling him how much he means to you. That's you all day."

Paityn laughed. "You're crazy."

"Baby, somehow you got it fucked up," Mom said.

I laughed. "Mom! When did you start using slang *and* cussing?" My mother had made a lot of money over the years in that Cussing Jar. Every time we'd said a curse word, we had to drop money in the jar. The amounts had grown as we'd aged and by the time we were in high school, we'd been stuffing dollars in that jar. Needless to say, she'd purchased a lot of clothes and handbags with that money. "And the term is got *me* fucked up."

"Mom is learning all of the new terms from Raven," Bliss said. "I'm proud of her for moving from the Eighties into this century."

"I'll help you out, Mom," Dallas offered. "In this case, Blake could've said 'Lennox got me fucked up' or you could've told her this: 'Blake, you got *me* fucked up.'"

"Ah." Mom tapped her chin. "I'll do better next time." She gave Dallas a high five. "Anyway, sometimes I wonder where we went wrong with you all."

"That's messed up, Mom," Paityn said.

"I didn't mean it in a bad way," my mother explained. "I just meant we've done our best to show you kids how freeing it is to love someone with everything in you. When I married your father, we vowed to do that for our kids, because we didn't see it from our parents. And we did that because we wanted all of you to believe in romantic love, in the unconditional love between spouses."

"I think you and Dad did a great job," Bliss said.

Mom patted Bliss' knee. "Thanks, baby." She looked at me. "Blake, please don't sabotage your chance at forever because you're scared."

Tears burned my eyes and tickled my nose. But this time I let them fall. "I always wonder if he'll get tired of me, that he'll realize I'm too jaded for him. It's easier to walk away from a bad relationship than to love someone so much…" My voice cracked. "And they leave you."

"You can't think like that," Paityn said. "You'll never be happy waiting on someone to leave you."

"I think you're so used to having control in every relationship that you're flipping out because you can't control Lennox," Dallas suggested.

"Not just that," Bliss cut in, "you've realized you can't control your feelings for him, either."

My feelings for Lennox had overwhelmed me for quite some time, and they just kept growing every day—whenever I looked into his eyes, every time he kissed me, any time we made love. I'd lost myself in him and it wasn't a bad feeling; it was actually liberating.

"Babe, I love you so much. You're my fighter. You've fought for your sisters, for your brothers, for us, for yourself. How about you try fighting for Lennox? Because I think you'd do yourself more harm by letting him walk away than letting him love you."

I wiped my eyes. "You're right. I'm not used to losing control, and it's…hard."

"It's okay to admit something's hard for you," Mom said. "But don't tell us. You need to be having this conversation with Lennox."

My watch buzzed. I peered at the face. "Bliss, can you give me my phone? It's Jace."

Bliss grabbed my phone from a nearby lounger and handed it to me.

"Hello?" I answered.

"Blake?" Jace called.

"Yes. What's up?"

"It's Lennox."

My stomach tightened. Gripping my phone, I asked, "What is it?"

"There was a fire."

I sat up, nearly losing my balance and falling into the water. It was only Paityn's steady hand on my arm that held me upright. "Is he okay?"

"The doctors are treating him for burns and severe smoke inhalation. They're optimistic, but we don't know the extent of the damage yet. You should come."

I tossed the phone to Bliss, and she immediately started asking Jace more questions. Jumping off the floater, I swam to the edge of the pool and climbed out, sprinting into the house to pack my bags. Because the only thing I cared about in that moment was getting to Lennox. I'd wasted so much time on bullshit, and it was time to make it right. It was time to tell him how much he meant to me. And I prayed to God it wasn't too late.

Chapter 13

THE WAY LOVE GOES

Lennox

he confusion, Julia's screams, the suffocating smoke, the heat of the flames, the excruciating pain, and the smell of burnt flesh had haunted me in my dreams. I couldn't think about what I would lose in the fire. I couldn't take time to grab my favorite books or my artwork or my photos. I had to focus on getting her out of there. I remembered spotting her on the ground, pinned down by a large piece of wood. I remembered pulling her from under it and picking her up. I remembered other people, students trying to help me, trying to grab things. I remember struggling to breathe and feeling like I wasn't going to make it. I remembered thinking about Blake, wondering if my parents and sisters would be okay without me. I remembered emerging from the building and the sting of the air against my skin. Then, everything had gone black.

Since then, my world consisted of nurses, doctors, oxygen masks, police officers, and beeping machines. My family had been steady, holding vigil in my hospital room as the doctors treated me. Luckily, it turned out not to be as bad as they'd originally thought. And thanks to the quick treatment, the doctors were hopeful that, if there was scarring, it would be minimal.

The damage to the building was also minimal. The firefighters had been able to put the fire out fairly quickly, and the presence of an accelerant on the scene was a clear indication it had been arson.

My mother's voice called to me. "Lennox?" She squeezed my arm, the one that hadn't been burned. "Baby?"

I opened my eyes. "Mom." I coughed, wincing at the pain shooting through my chest. I hadn't talked much since they'd brought me in, because it hurt. Everything hurt.

She held out a cup of water. "Drink some of this."

I took a sip of water and burrowed into the pillow. "How is Julia?"

My mom's eyes softened. "She's going to be okay. Her burns were more severe than yours, but the doctors expect a full recovery."

Squeezing my eyes closed, I tried to forget about her screams, about the terrified look in her eyes. "I'm glad."

"Jace stopped by," Mom told me. "It was Dory who set the fire. Apparently, she turned herself in late last night. Your father is livid. He's pushing for attempted murder."

As much as I'd hoped she'd move on and get the help she needed, the revelation didn't shock me. I'd had a feeling it was her from the beginning, from the moment I'd found out the fire had originated in my office.

"Vaughn and Emerie will be here soon," my mom continued.

I shook my head. "They don't need to come. They should be packing for their move."

"I couldn't talk them out of it, and I wouldn't. They love you." She placed her hand over my heart. "We all do, babe. We love you so much." Leaning down, she kissed my cheek. "Praise God you're going to be okay. The whole church was praying."

"Tell everyone I said thank you."

"I will." She smiled down at me. "There's someone who wants to see you."

Meeting her gaze, I frowned. "Who?"

"Me?" I looked at the door, surprised to see Blake standing there, a bouquet of flowers in her hand and a tentative smile on her lips. "I couldn't figure out what to bring you, so I picked up these manly flowers on my way here from the airport."

Chuckling, I said, "Manly flowers?"

Blake inched closer to me. The tears swimming in her eyes were unmistakable. She'd been crying. "I probably should've went with a plant, huh?"

"It doesn't matter. I don't care about flowers or plants. I just want you."

My mom sniffed. "That's so sweet."

"Mom?"

Mom blinked. "Oh, I'll just leave you two alone." She hugged Blake. "I'm so glad you're here," she whispered before quietly exiting the room.

Blake set the flowers down on a table and grabbed my hand, burying her face in my palm and kissing it. "I was so scared," she confessed. "Good thing my mom flew back with me. I was a wreck—I must've cried the entire way here." She laughed. "See what you did to me?"

The sight of her standing there, so vulnerable, was

overwhelming. I wanted to hold her, to assure her everything would be okay. But I still wasn't sure where we stood. "You came back."

"I'm so sorry, Lennox."

I closed my eyes and let her apology wash over me. My father's words to me flitted through my mind. We needed to talk before we did anything else. "Blake, we need—"

"No, Lennox," she interrupted. "Let me finish. I'm not one to act like I didn't fuck up. Because I did." Her chin trembled and she let out a shaky breath. "I'm going to be very transparent with you, okay?"

"Okay."

"If I start crying again, don't tell anyone."

Laughing, I promised, "Your secret is safe with me."

"I act all brave and shit, but, um…I'm scared to death of us."

"Why?"

"You are so good, patient, and sweet. And you accept me—all of my jaded and petty and dramatic ways. You've never tried to change me or make me feel wrong for being who I am. You see me, everything that's ugly and stubborn and not fun—and you still want me. You challenge me, you push me. You make me feel safe."

In my wildest dreams, I'd never expected Blake to be so raw, so open with me. I loved this side of her. I loved that she felt safe enough to say these things. I loved that she'd flown home to see me. I loved that she'd apologized. *I love her*.

"You're like a dryer sheet."

I frowned. "What?"

"You know how clothes are wrinkled and static-y and stiff before you put them in the dryer?"

"Right," I said.

"Dryer sheets make everything soft and smooth. That's you. That's what you do for me."

"O…kay."

"I love you."

I lifted my eyes, locked my gaze on her. "You do?"

She nodded. "Yeah, I do. I love you so much, so big that it scares me."

"I'd never hurt you."

"You could. Because *my* heart…it's *your* heart."

I squeezed her hand and tugged her forward. Holding her hand to my heart, I said, "And my heart is your heart."

Blake closed her eyes. "It is?"

"Yes, Blake. I love you too. I love everything about you. I want nights with you, mornings next to you, meals together, vacations… I want everything. All of it, all of you." She bent down, resting her forehead against mine. "I want to take this leap with you. And I want you to jump with me and know everything isn't going to be perfect."

Caressing my face with her palms, she kissed me. "It feels perfect to me."

Wrapping my arm around her, I pulled her into a kiss again. I circled her nose with mine. "It does, doesn't it? You in?"

"All in, Lennox."

"No more trips without notice."

"I promise." She climbed into bed with me. When I winced, she hopped out of the bed. "Are you okay? Did I hurt you?"

"No. Come here."

She bit down on her lip. "You're lying."

"I'm fine."

"Are you sure?"

"Blake, get your ass in this bed." She tried again, this

time slower. I pulled her closer. "This is better." She rested her hand on my heart again. It felt good to hold her, to know she was mine.

"Lennox?"

"Yes?"

Peering at me, she said, "I didn't expect you. But I'm glad I broke into your house and stole your vase."

I laughed. "It's definitely a story to tell our kids."

"Kids?"

"Be quiet." I searched her eyes. "You're definitely unexpected, Blake Young."

"And you were definitely trouble—good and bad. I love you, Professor Cole."

"Love you too."

Blake

Two months later

"I'M STILL MAD AT YOU?"

Lennox brushed his lips over mine. "I love you," he murmured against my mouth.

"Ugh…you get on my nerves."

He peppered kisses over my jawline up to my ear, nipping my ear lobe. "I love your smile."

Oh, God. My boyfriend was too damn sexy for his own good—or *my* own good. "You're so wrong for this."

"I love your body." His lips were everywhere—on my shoulders, above my breasts. "I love your mind."

I sagged against the bed. "You'd better stop. We have so much to do."

"I love that you're so damn petty."

I laughed. "You're playing hard ball."

"No, baby."

Pulling back, I said, "No?"

He shook his head. "I don't believe I stuttered." He sucked my bottom lip into his mouth. One of us moaned. I couldn't be sure if it was me or him. I didn't care. "Tell me you love me," he commanded softly.

"I love you." I kissed him. "I'm still mad at you, though."

"Why?"

"Because if it wasn't for your happy ass, we wouldn't be having this housewarming party tonight."

Lennox laughed. "You're going to blame this on me?"

"It's your fault. Everyone knows I don't like people all up in my space, especially nosy people. Your mother's church friends ask me all the time when we're getting married."

He leaned his forehead against my shoulder. "You can't blame them for being happy for us."

I arched a brow. "Oh, yes I can. Last week at the pantry, Sister Brown cornered me near the potatoes and asked if we were planning on having a big family."

"What did you tell her?"

Rolling my eyes, I said, "I told her to ask the Lord."

His mouth fell open. "Blake."

"What? She said she was praying for us, so I told her the Lord knew when and if we were getting married so she should pray about it."

"I'm sure that went over well," he muttered.

"Actually, it did. She walked away and didn't come back."

He shook his head. "I'm speechless."

"It's okay. She probably won't even remember next time. She forgot potatoes aren't fruit. And she forgot her dentures."

Lennox cracked up. "I'm done with this conversation."

I brushed my finger over the long scar on his arm. Lennox had healed quite well from the fire. He'd had no long-term complications, and the doctors were hopeful his scars would fade sooner than later. Julia had also made a remarkable recovery, but suffered from post-traumatic stress syndrome and had recently announced her retirement from the university. I knew it bothered Lennox to know someone was hurt because Dory couldn't handle rejection. Sometimes he still had nightmares about the fire. And all I could do was hold him, tell him I was there for him, assure him I wouldn't leave him.

As for Dory, she'd been indicted on attempted murder, arson, and aggravated stalking. Lennox would never get back what he'd lost in the fire—the books, his art, his photos, his favorite jacket. But I was glad he was still here, still breathing, still alive. And I hoped justice would be served at the trial later in the year.

"I'd better get up." I scooted to the edge of the bed and pulled on one of Lennox's shirts. Standing, I stretched, loving the way his gaze raked over my body. "Stop looking at me like that, Lennox."

I popped him with a pillow and raced out of our bedroom. It didn't take him long to catch me, but only because I wanted him to. He scooped me up in his arms and carried me the rest of the way to the kitchen. Empty boxes were sitting on the floor, ready to be broken down.

Dishes were stacked on the counter, waiting to be put in cabinets.

He set me atop of the counter and pulled the shirt off, tossing it behind us. "I haven't had you up here yet." Lennox sucked one of my nipples into his mouth.

I shivered, trying to keep my mind on what had to be done before the first guest arrived. After Lennox had been released from the hospital, we'd decided we didn't want to waste any more time. And since we loved sleeping together so much, we figured we should just do it permanently.

Things had gone fast from there. My cousin, Linc, had announced he was moving to the DMV area, and Lennox and I had offered to buy their four-bedroom home. Bliss had stayed in my house, and Lennox had put his house up for sale. It was kismet, meant to be.

I moaned as he licked his way to my pussy. "Lennox, we really need to clean up around here."

He stopped and stood to his full height. "You're right. I'd better start breaking down those boxes."

"After you finish," I said.

He smirked, dropped to his knees, and sucked my clit into his mouth. I was lost in the haze of desire, calling out his name over and over again until an orgasm crested within me. I tripped over the edge, letting out a strangled cry.

My back hit the cold countertop. "So much trouble," I murmured.

Lennox stood again and kissed me. "You love trouble."

"I love you."

"That never gets old." Smiling, he handed me his shirt. "Put this on."

I folded my arms over my chest. "Why? You started something I want to finish."

"Later." He picked up a box and studied it. "What's this?"

"Paityn sent it. She told me not to open it until we were alone."

Frowning, Lennox shook it. "Think it's more of *That Ish?*"

That Ish was my sister's top seller, a clit cream that had men and women going crazy for more. "I don't think so. She said it's new."

He eyed me. "We're alone now."

I smirked. "But you said we had to clean."

"And we will—after we see what's in here." He opened the box and pulled out a smaller box.

Leaning in, I read the label. I glanced at him, noting the wicked gleam in his eyes. "Oh, no."

"Obviously, she wants us to try it."

I hopped off the counter and backed away from him. "Lennox, we can't. That's too much. We have shit to do."

He inched closer to me, peeling the plastic wrap from the smaller box. "I think we have time."

"No." I shook my head. "We can't."

"You trust me?" he asked.

I nodded. "I do, but…"

"Alright then. Go get in the shower."

Dammit. I loved when he tossed out dirty commands.

He pulled out a small thing of lubricant and opened it. "Now," he ordered.

I eyed him as he coated the *Booty Up* butt plug with gel. I ran to the bathroom, turned on the shower, and stepped inside. A moment later, he joined me.

The warm water felt good on my back, and so did he. I bent over, gasping when I felt his fingers against my butt. I moaned when he pushed one inside my hole, spreading more lubricant there.

I stared at him over my shoulder. He seemed transfixed on my body, his hungry eyes devouring me. My legs shook as I waited. Finally, with his gaze locked on mine, Lennox inserted the toy slowly.

"Oh, shit," I breathed.

"So beautiful," he whispered, gripping my hips. "So mine." His finger brushed against my clit, and I purred. "I'll never stop wanting you, baby."

"Please," I begged. "Now."

Pressing his erection against my pussy, he entered me. "Damn, baby," he growled.

"Oh, God. Oh, damn." I lost my train of thought, unable to concentrate on anything but the amazing feeling of him inside me. I was captivated by him, by us together. Closing my eyes, I savored every emotion in that moment —trust, adoration, desire, love.

Sensations almost too much to bear overloaded me, making me ache for him, for more of this. As he moved, he whispered how he couldn't get enough of me, how he never wanted to stop making love to me, how much he wanted me, how much he loved me. And I was on the edge, so close I thought I'd explode from the pleasure. Soon, his pace increased, grew more frenzied as he pounded into me. I could do nothing but hold on for dear life, because I wasn't going to last. Sure enough, I succumbed to a delicious orgasm. He gripped my chin, kissing me hard as he fell over with me.

I couldn't move even if I wanted to. Then, I felt his hands against my body, smelled my soap as he washed my sensitive skin. His touch was so gentle, so tender, I wanted to weep.

When he finished, he picked me up and carried me to the bedroom, where he towel-dried me and deposited me into the bed. Leaning down, he brushed his lips over mine. "Sleep, baby. I'll wake you up in an hour."

One hour turned into four hours, and I jumped up, panicked we weren't going to be ready for tonight. I slid out of the bed and rushed into the living room. Scanning the area, I was surprised to find it clean. No boxes, nothing out of place. But…*where is Lennox?*

The door opened, and Lennox walked into the house with several grocery bags. When he saw me, he smiled. "You're finally up." He brushed past me and put the bags on the counter. I peeked in one of them, spotting some of the items from the list I'd made earlier.

"You went shopping without me?" I asked.

"And I hired a chef."

Duke stepped into the house with more bags. "What's up, B?"

My mouth fell open. "You're here. I didn't think you were coming."

Grinning, Duke set his bags on the counter and washed his hands. "I never miss a party. And Len told me you needed food, so here I am."

"Baby, you… I can't believe you did this."

"The man loves you, punk. Go sit down somewhere so we can get shit done before Dallas comes and tries to boss us around. Better yet, why don't you put on some clothes?"

My gaze dropped to my bare legs. Luckily, I'd thought to put on one of Lennox's shirts. My face burned. "Yeah, I'll do that."

An hour later, my siblings were starting to trickle in. The first to arrive was Asa, followed by Bliss, then Dexter. We were setting up the food trays when Dallas barged in.

"What the hell is wrong with you?" Dex asked.

"Good question," Asa murmured.

I frowned. I'd never seen my sister like this. Her hair

was a mess on top of her head, she wore no makeup, and her clothes were crooked. "Dallas, what's up with your outfit? And that hair? Girl, why are you looking like this?"

Dallas let out a frustrated sigh and stomped over to the counter. She smacked down a piece of paper. "Here."

Grabbing the card stock, I read it. My eyes widened. "I'm so confused."

"I'm getting married." I opened my mouth to speak, but she covered it with her hand. "No questions. I don't want to talk about it." She glanced at all of us. "I mean it. Not a word."

I stared at her, slack-jawed. I had questions, but my parents chose that exact moment to show up.

"Dallas?" I said.

"I need clothes and makeup. Fix my hair." And she disappeared down the hall.

I met Lennox's concerned gaze and shrugged. Then, I followed her.

THE PARTY WAS A HUGE SUCCESS. Good food, good people. Our families got along well. Mrs. Cole and my mother hit it off wonderfully. Our fathers had already scheduled a round of golf. And our siblings… I was certain if Emerie or Dana were single, my mannish brothers would've tried to holla at both of them. And Lennox? He was perfect.

As everything wound down, he pulled me to him, kissing me softly.

I wiped my gloss off his lips. "Thank you."

"For what?"

"For loving me the way you do. I didn't think I could be this happy." Lennox had checked every box for me. He was everything I never thought I needed—sincere, sexy, intelligent, funny, patient. Oh, and that smile. He owned my heart, and I wouldn't have it any other way. "I told you…you are so much trouble."

He laughed. "I'll be that. For you. I love you."

"Forever?"

"Always." He circled my nose with his.

It was a move I would've once considered corny and uncalled for, but I loved when *he* did it. "I love you too. And I love my family. But I'm ready for them to go so you can teach me another naughty lesson, Professor Cole."

Epilogue

FREE

Blake

Sometime Later

"*O*pen them."

Smiling, I opened my eyes. A small box sat on the table. I looked at Lennox, backing away from him. "What's that?"

"Your gift."

My birthday weekend had been a whirlwind, starting from the orgasm he'd blessed me with yesterday morning to the surprise trip to Turks and Caicos yesterday afternoon to the tiny gifts he'd presented me along the way.

We'd arrived at the all-inclusive resort and had hidden away in our secluded villa for the rest of the day, making love on the sundeck and in the private pool and on the beach. Today was the first time we'd actually done something outside of our perfect haven. Lennox had arranged for us to enjoy sailing, snorkeling, and other water activities. We'd danced on the beach and had dinner under the stars. Now, we were relaxing with bourbon and cigars—and that damn box. A small box. A box that looked too much like a ring box.

"What is it?" I asked again.

"Your gift," he repeated. "Open it."

Life with Lennox had been better than I'd ever hoped it'd be. I loved him more today than I did yesterday, and I was sure I'd love him more tomorrow than I did today.

Months ago, I'd committed a crime, had gotten arrested, and had met the love of my life in the same night. Everything for me changed that cold January day, and I wouldn't trade him for anything.

Our life together was never boring, and I didn't question his motives or spend my moments looking for a way out. I just wanted him. But that box…

"Tell me what it is," I pressed.

He pried my palm open and set the box in my hand. "Blake, open that damn gift."

"Are you proposing?"

"If I was, you just ruined it."

"Are you? Because if you are—"

"Baby, stop. It's your birthday. I have one last gift for you. I need you to stop playin' and open that shit."

Sighing, I puffed my cigar before I finally opened the box. But it wasn't a ring. I lifted the cigar cutter and studied it. And an unfamiliar emotion welled up inside me —disappointment. Shocked the hell out of me, because…*did I want it to be a ring?*

The question didn't have an easy answer. Marriage hadn't crossed my mind. I was simply enjoying Lennox, enjoying our life together. Yet, when I'd thought it was a ring, the idea of marrying him had been seared on my brain. Now, it was all I could think about, and he'd given me a damn cigar cutter.

"Do you like it?" Lennox asked.

"Sure," I lied.

"You always want to use mine, so I figured I'd buy you one of your own."

"Great," I chirped, dropping the cigar cutter into the box. I kissed him. "Love it, baby." Picking up my glass, I downed the contents and sunk back into my chair.

A smirk formed on Lennox's perfect lips. "Baby?"

"Hm?"

"What did you think was in that box?"

I hunched a shoulder. "Nothing. I mean… I didn't know. That's why I asked," I added under my breath.

"Would you have liked something like this?" He held out another box, this time an *open* box—with a gorgeous ring inside.

"Oh," I breathed, looking at the cushion-cut diamond. "Lennox, you…?"

"Love you," he finished for me. "I love you and I can't even think about life without you. I don't want to. Marry me."

"Dammit." I pointed at him as tears spilled down my cheek. "Don't tell anyone I cried."

"I told you…all your secrets are safe with me."

Biting down on my lip, I nodded. "Then, yes. I'll marry you."

Lennox slipped the ring on my finger, scooped me up, and carried me into our villa. And when we made love as a newly engaged couple, I knew I'd never want anything or anyone else. For the rest of my life.

Coming Summer 2021

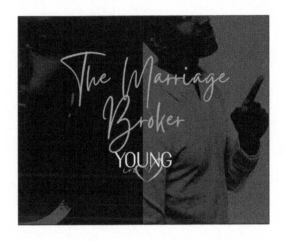

An offer and a wedding… Dallas Young has a decision to make.
This time, there's no turning back.

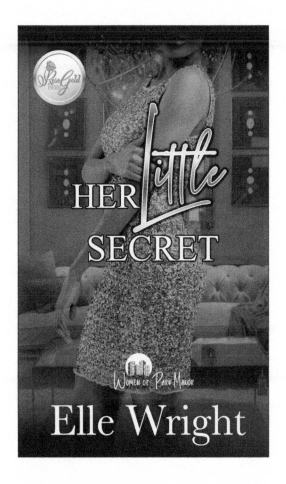

HER *Little* SECRET

WOMEN OF PARK MANOR

Elle Wright

Sex therapist, Paityn Young, couldn't get much sex in her city. So she developed her own line of naughty toys to get the job done. Now, she's bringing her talent to LA, hoping to launch her new company. Only her new business consultant has her thinking about more than just her product line.

As a favor to his boss, Bishop Lang agrees to help Paityn develop her new business. The only thing he knows about her is that she's off limits, but the moment he sees her, he realizes staying away might be harder than he thought. And his own personal journey may take a backseat to the blossoming relationship developing between them.

Excerpt: Her Little Secret

WOMEN OF PARK MANOR

*I*f Paityn could ban two words, *fuck* and *shit* would be it. One made her think of toilets. The other? Well, let's just say she didn't need to be reminded of something she hadn't been blessed to do in years. And for the last ten minutes, she'd listened to her sister string those same two words together in varying combinations.

"Girl! Enough!" Paityn shouted, cutting her sister off mid-curse. "Road rage is really a thing. Get help." Pulling two sets of new sheets out of the dryer, she walked into one of the spare bedrooms and dropped the bedding on the mattress.

"Shit, I need to vent," Blake yelled. "It's your fuckin' fault I'm in this predicament. Michigan traffic doesn't make me want to kill someone."

Unable to help herself, Paityn giggled at her younger sister's antics. "You're a mess."

"Hey, I can only be me," Blake said.

The loud blare of the car horn followed by another colorful curse had her shaking her head in amusement. Some things would never change. Trump was still an asshole, she still couldn't eat beans to save her life, and Blake Young still had a potty mouth.

"I'm hanging up," Paityn told her sister. "I have stuff to do before you get here."

When "the brats" told her they were coming for a visit during the Memorial Day holiday, Paityn was ecstatic. Since her cross-country move, she'd seen her sisters countless times thanks to technology. But air kisses and virtual hugs didn't replace real face-to-face contact.

"Paityn?" Bliss called through the phone. She noted the rasp in her baby sister's voice, as if she'd been sleeping. "Are you making something for dinner? I'm hungry."

"Yes, ma'am." She walked the other set of sheets to the third bedroom and dumped them on the bed. "I'm making reservations. At this new Cuban restaurant Rissa told me about."

"Damn," Bliss muttered. "Will you at least cook breakfast in the morning?"

"You're so greedy," Blake said. "You just ate a whole foot-long sub and half of mine."

"I can't help it," Bliss shouted.

"I'm starting to think you're only here because you want me to cook for you." Paityn hurried to the kitchen and opened the oven. The homemade peach cobbler she'd prepared was almost done, Blake's favorite.

"No, I'm here because I miss you," Bliss said, just as Blake shouted another obscenity at a driver.

"That's good to hear." She also checked the macaroni and cheese baking in the bottom oven. *My favorite.*

"I wish Dallas could have come," Bliss mused. "I tried to get her to cancel her plans."

Paityn lifted the top off the pot on the stovetop, stirring the mustard and turnip greens a bit before she turned down the heat. "I do, too. But I'm not mad at her for taking a vacation out of the country. It's about time." She glanced at the Instant Pot on the countertop, noting the remaining time on the pulled pork, Bliss' favorite.

The truth? She did have reservations for dinner and dancing. Tomorrow. But, tonight, she also wanted to spoil her sisters a little. And it had been a while since she'd cooked anything of substance.

Growing up the second oldest child of a world-renowned couple, known for mending relationships and teaching others to parent, had a unique set of challenges. Partly because it was hard to live in her parents' shadows, but mostly because there were eight of them. Yes, Stewart and Victoria Young had eight damn children—willingly and happily. Paityn was the responsible sister, the oldest daughter, always offering a plate of food, a hand to hold, and a shoulder to cry on.

"Duke is pissed you didn't invite him," Bliss said.

Paityn laughed, thinking of the phone call she'd received from her brother earlier that morning. "I didn't invite y'all."

"But you're glad we're here," Blake added.

"I am, but I'm hanging up. I gave the concierge your names, so you should be able to come up without any problems. Don't kill anybody, Blake. See you soon."

Paityn ended the call after her sisters screamed good-bye. Shaking her head, she turned the dishwasher on and poured a glass of wine. When the oven timer went off, she pulled the dessert out and set it atop the island. The smell of peaches and cinnamon wafted to her nose and she resisted the urge to taste the cobbler.

She scanned the notes she'd jotted down earlier that day. The clitoral cream she'd hoped to perfect had been harder than she originally thought. Between her work as a sex therapist and her science background, it should have been a no brainer. Yet, she'd failed to even achieve the big "O" for the first two batches she'd made. Biting her thumbnail, she pondered her choice of ingredients. Maybe she'd used too much sodium benzoate?

Paityn scribbled an idea on the notepad and eyed the prototype she'd created. It was the fifth dildo she'd created and, by far, the best. She couldn't wait to show Blake and Bliss, which was why it was out in the open and not in her makeshift office-slash-lab.

Once Paityn had decided every woman needed a big ass dick, the wheels started spinning and a business idea formed. Paityn knew there were other sex aids on the market, entire stores dedicated to the business of pleasure, but she'd jumped in anyway. Now she was preparing to pitch her brand of sexual enhancement products.

When her stomach growled, Paityn glanced over at the peach cobbler. *One spoonful won't hurt.* She grabbed a wooden spoon and scooped a heaping helping out of the pan. Before she knew it one bite turned into two. Then, three. *Oh my God.* Four.

Fortunately, the knock on the door interrupted her greedy moment. She licked the spoon as she headed toward the door. She'd figured it would be at least thirty minutes before her sisters arrived. The airport was less than fifteen miles away, but it almost always took more than thirty minutes to get there in the infuriating 405 traffic.

She wiped a hand against her black leggings and opened the door. "You're her—"

Only it wasn't Blake or Bliss at the door. It wasn't even Rissa. No, the very *male* visitor standing there, his fist poised to knock again, was someone she didn't know. But damn, he was someone she probably *should* get to know.

Swallowing, she plastered a grin on her face and hoped

she looked presentable. "Hi." When he didn't answer immediately, she swallowed. *Maybe the hottie is a creeper?* But it wasn't like she was in some random apartment building. The concierge didn't just let anyone come up to the top floor.

The stranger's eyes dropped to her mouth and she absently wiped it with her sleeve, hoping she didn't have peach cobbler crust on her face.

"Can I help you?" she asked.

He blinked and then blessed her with the sexiest smile she'd ever seen up close. Pretty white teeth, adorably deep dimples, and beautiful creases framing full lips.

"I'm sorry. My name is Bishop." He held out a hand, presumably for her to shake it.

Her gaze dropped to it, noted his long fingers and clean fingernails, but she made no move to touch him. *Not yet.*

"I work at Pure Talent," he continued. "Jax Starks told me about you."

Paityn's eyes widened. "Oh, yeah. Bishop Lang."

Why is my voice so high? Probably because when her godfather told her he wanted her to meet one of the best legal minds on his team, she'd assumed it was an old, graying grandfather. A man that golfed on his off days and spent weekends at some highbrow country club drinking Burnt Martinis or scotch on the rocks. Not this fine ass man with smooth dark skin and a body that made her want to sing, "Do me, Baby". Because she was sure he'd be able to handle the job in a way no one ever had before. *Focus, Paityn.*

"Yes, that's me." His tongue darted out to wet his lips. "I live in the building and figured I'd come up and introduce myself."

Unable to turn away, she nodded. "Right. I think Uncle Jax did tell me that."

Briefly, she wondered if this was even a good idea, considering she couldn't stop staring at him. How would she be able to concentrate on business? But she trusted her godfather's judgment because he had never failed her and always had her best interests at heart.

From an early age, Paityn learned that blood didn't make family. And it was because of relationships like the one her father and Jax Starks had. The two men had grown up near each other in Detroit, Michigan and had even pledged the same fraternity. They were brothers in every sense of the word, even though they were born to different parents. Jax was her godfather, but he was also her "uncle".

She finally stepped aside. "Come in."

He followed her toward the kitchen. "Peach cobbler." The low groan that followed hit her right in the gut—or lower. "Smells good."

She gulped down the rest of her wine and dropped the wooden spoon into the sink. "I'm making dinner for my sisters." She turned the greens off and tried to recall everything her godfather had told her about Bishop. Clearly, she'd missed some things that he'd said. "I thought you were going to be out of town until next week?"

"I got back a little early."

Paityn leaned against the counter, meeting his intense gaze once again. "Cobbler?" she asked.

He looked down at the dessert and swallowed visibly. Nodding slowly, he said, "No."

Paityn frowned, surprised at his answer. Normally, a nod meant yes. "You sure? Because you look like you want some."

"I'm sure." He glanced at the pan again, before he looked up at her.

Tilting her head, she studied him. Something was preventing him from eating her cobbler. Did she want to know what? *Or who?* The need to know more welled up inside her. *It's the nature of my job to ask questions.* It wasn't his arms. Or the muscles stretching against the t-shirt he wore. The fact that he may be eating someone else's pie didn't bother her either. Well, not really.

Instead of probing further, she decided a change of subject was best. "Uncle Jax tells me you work in the business development department," she said. "But what else should I know?" Okay, so her attempt to sound professional came out more sultry than businesslike.

"What do mean?" he asked.

Clearing her throat, she added, "Because if we're going to work together, I'd like to learn a little more about your ass." Her eyes widened. "I mean, your experience?"

He chuckled. "I can give you the long version, or the short version."

Hello, sexual innuendo. She really did need to get some. Everything about this man and this interaction made her mind sink to the gutter. Paityn scratched her neck. "How about we start with where you're from?"

"Long Beach."

She opened the refrigerator and pulled out two bottles of water and offered him one. "Law school?"

"Berkeley." He took the water and twisted off the cap. "I've worked for the agency for fifteen years, and I've been instrumental in negotiating several business deals for agency clients. Jax has also entrusted me with many of his personal business matters."

"Good. What has he told you about me?"

His mouth curved into a smile. "He mentioned you were important to him and that I should take care of you."

She bit down on her lip. "I mean, about my business idea."

"Only that you were a sex therapist looking to start a new venture."

Paityn grinned, pleased that he didn't seem uncomfortable with her occupation like some men. "That's true. Did he tell you anything else?"

Bishop raised a brow. "No. I assume you will tell me the details."

"Right. I'll send you the draft of my proposal." She slid her notebook over and jotted down a note to herself. "I probably should have done this as soon as he gave me your email address, but I didn't want to interrupt your vacation. I know we always say we won't check emails on vacation, but we always do."

Ha barked out a laugh. "I don't disagree with that."

"Let me know when you're free to meet." She closed the notebook. "I have appointments during the day, but I'm usually free in the evenings." Paityn conducted her sessions online, via video chat or text therapy, which she'd found to be a great alternative to in-office therapy. Most of her clients loved the convenience and it allowed her to work from the comfort of her home, wherever that was.

"I'll check my calendar and get back to you. I have your numbers."

"Great. You'll have an email tonight. Not that I don't think you wouldn't read my proposal before we meet, but you definitely should. And preferably not in the office. In front of people."

The last thing she wanted was for a picture of her prototype to flash across his screen while he had someone in his office. That would be embarrassing, for him and for her.

Bishop frowned. "Why do I feel like I should be scared?"

Paityn laughed. "Because you should." She waggled her eyebrows.

"Now, I'm curious. Maybe you should give me a hint?"

"I would, but—" A knock on the door interrupted her explanation. "Excuse me. I have to get the door."

She ran to the door and opened it. Before she could say anything, Blake and Bliss surrounded her, hugging her tightly. Paityn wasn't overly emotional, but it felt good to hug her sisters, and she held on for longer than normal.

Finally pulling back, she smiled at the twins, noting the tears standing in Bliss' eyes. She brushed her cheek. "Don't cry."

"Please don't." Blake rolled her eyes. "It hasn't even been a month. Get it together."

"Leave me alone." Bliss elbowed Blake. "At least I don't have a black heart."

Paityn giggled. "Get in here." She pulled one of the rolling suitcases inside. "Are you hungry?"

Bliss patted her stomach. "You know it."

"I thought you weren't cooking," Blake said.

Paityn led them around the corner into the open living room area. "You know I wasn't going to let you come here without making your favorites."

"So, no Cuban food?" Blake asked. "Because I had my mouth set... Oooh wee. This place is gorgeous. Floor-to-ceiling windows, stunning artwork. And I love the color scheme. Everything just flows. Uncle Jax is doing big things."

Bishop glanced up from his phone and stood. "Hi."

Blake bit down on her thumbnail. "And apparently so are you," she muttered under her breath.

"Who is that, sissy?" Bliss whispered.

"And tell me he has a brother," Blake added.

Paityn rolled her eyes. "Shut up." She introduced them to Bishop. "He's an attorney at Pure Talent and he's helping me with my business."

"Oh, so you're helping her with the Big Ass D?" Blake asked, a wicked gleam in her eyes.

Bishop blinked. "Excuse me?"

Paityn glared at Blake. "He doesn't know about that yet," she said between clenched teeth. Leave it to her little sister to embarrass the hell out of her. "I'm sorry, Bishop. Don't mind her."

"Is that peach cobbler?" Blake asked.

"Yes," Bliss answered from the kitchen. She lifted the top off the pan. "And there's greens. And it smells like pulled pork. Yum."

Paityn shrugged when Bishop met her eyes. "Sisters."

"Right," he said. "I should probably get going, let you visit with your sisters. We'll talk."

"I'll walk you out."

He waved her off. "You don't have to."

"I do." Paityn walked him to the door. "Thanks for stopping by. I'm looking forward to working with you." She finally reached out to shake his hand.

When their palms met, she couldn't help but notice how the contact flooded her with warmth, from the tips of her fingers to her shoulders and throughout her body.

"It's good to meet you, Paityn." His husky, low voice made her want to lean into him.

She didn't, though. Slipping her hand from his, she nodded. "Right."

"I'll talk to you soon."

She nodded again. Because apparently she couldn't form any words.

Once he was safely outside the door, she exhaled. If every interaction with him ended with a handshake that somehow felt more like a kiss or a tender caress against her bare skin... *I'm definitely in trouble.*

Acknowledgments

First, I want to thank God. He's everything I need.

Jason, you're my hero. Thank you for loving me the way you do. I love you so much.

Sherelle... GIRL!! Sometimes I need to *see* it to believe it. The bomb covers you created brought my vision to life! Thanks for encouraging me to actually write it; for giving me good support, good titles, and good advice. I'm forever grateful for you.

Tash and Kaia, I still remember what I was doing when I shared this idea with you. I also remember how excited you both were. Thank you for being my biggest cheerleaders! Love you both!

Sheryl, you already know! You always know what to say, what to do. I can't thank you enough for everything!

Midnight, Shavonna, Loretta, Matysha... You all are amazing! Thank you for the feedback, the laughs, the support. I truly appreciate you!

A special shout-out to the awesome readers , bloggers, and writers that I've met on this journey. Thanks for your support. I appreciate you!

Connect with Elle!

Subscribe to my Newsletter
New Releases, Upcoming projects, and Freebies!

On Facebook,
Join my cocktail lounge for exclusive updates, drink recipes,
and lots of fun!
bit.ly/EllesCocktailLounge

Visit my website: www.ellewright.com

Email me at info@ellewright.com

facebook.com/ellewrightauthor

twitter.com/LWrightAuthor

instagram.com/lwrightauthor

amazon.com/Elle-Wright/e/B00VMEWB78

Also by Elle Wright

Contemporary Romance

Edge of Scandal Series

The Forbidden Man

His All Night

Her Kind of Man

All He Wants for Christmas

Once Upon a Series

Beyond Forever (Once Upon a Bridesmaid)

Beyond Ever After (Once Upon a Baby)

Finding Cooper (Once Upon a Funeral)

Jacksons of Ann Arbor

It's Always Been You

Wherever You Are

Because Of You

All For You

Wellspring Series

Touched By You

Enticed By You

Pleasured By You

Pure Talent Series

The Way You Tempt Me

The Way You Hold Me

The Way You Love Me

Distinguished Gentlemen Series

The Closing Bid

Women of Park Manor

Her Little Secret

Carnivale Chronicles

Irresistible Temptation

New Year Bae-Solutions

One More Drink

Historical Romance

DECADES: A Journey of African American Romance

Made To Hold You (The 80s)

Suspense/Thriller

Basement Level 5: Never Scared

About the Author

There was never a time when Elle Wright wasn't about to start a book, wasn't already deep in a book—or had just finished one. She grew up believing in the importance of reading, and became a lover of all things romance when her mother gave her her first romance novel. She lives in Michigan.

Connect with Elle!
www.ellewright.com
info@ellewright.com

Made in the USA
Las Vegas, NV
21 May 2021